W9-CUL-597

'Ah, yes, the career.' Caspar arched an ironic eyebrow. **'How's it going, by the way?'**

'Fine, thank you,' Abbie snapped back, trying to ignore the sarcasm. 'Now, about…'

'Abbie, I can't stop to discuss anything now. I have a surgery to run.'

'Not for much longer,' she retaliated. 'I'm home now. I don't know what your plans are…' She stopped, hoping he'd tell her, but he didn't. He just sat there, still with that damned eyebrow quirked.

Carol Wood lives with her artist husband, her grown-up family and parents on the south coast of England. She has always taken an interest in medical matters, especially general practice and nursing in the community. Her hobbies are walking by the sea, watching wildlife and, of course, reading and writing romantic fiction.

Recent titles by the same author:

BACK IN HER BED
THE PATIENT DOCTOR*
THE HONOURABLE DOCTOR*

*Country Partners duo

HER PARTNER'S PASSION

BY
CAROL WOOD

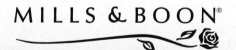

MILLS & BOON®

LT
WOO

First published in Great Britain 2002
Large Print edition 2002
Harlequin Mills & Boon Limited,
Eton House, 18-24 Paradise Road,
Richmond, Surrey TW9 1SR

© Carol Wood 2002

ISBN 0 263 17322 4

Set in Times Roman 15¾ on 16¾ pt.
17-1202-56594

Printed and bound in Great Britain
by Antony Rowe Ltd, Chippenham, Wiltshire

CHAPTER ONE

ABBIE woke with a start.

Even before her hand hit the snooze button, she realised she wasn't at home.

At least, not her LA home.

Her fingers grappled with the unfamiliar contours of her travelling clock and silenced the irritating buzz. A minute or two later she hauled herself up and stretched her legs in a pathetic attempt to wake up.

With her eyes closed, she drew her hair into a bunch at her neck. And waited.

Waited for recollection to dawn.

It came. Thick and fast, snaking itself round her ribs, constricting her breathing. What do you expect? she asked herself irritably. First morning back home. First morning in the house—*without Dad*.

'I'm OK,' she told herself, and carefully let out a breath. She lowered her shoulders and relaxed. 'I'm fine.' She sniffed loudly. 'So, Abbie Scott, what are you waiting for?'

Stumbling to the basin, she found her answer in the mirror. Grass green eyes drugged by sleep.

A wild tangle of auburn curls. A skin so pale, the freckles on her nose shone like beacons.

How long had she slept? she wondered, and glanced at her watch. Ten hours? She'd crashed out at seven. Hadn't surfaced since. She sighed disappointedly. So much for her resolution to tackle Caspar Darke last night.

She barely recalled having had supper with the man. He'd had to go out anyway. On a call, he'd said. The next thing she'd known, she'd been struggling to keep awake.

Obviously she hadn't.

Abbie yawned and stretched luxuriously. Had it really been six weeks ago when Caspar Darke had made that transatlantic call and told her of Dad's death? She had only registered him at first as her father's locum. A man with hidden depths, she'd decided on their first brief meeting two years ago, and had made a note never to investigate them.

A shower was what she needed and she braced herself as she stood under it. Mountain stream cold, as usual. Dad had never fixed the boiler. And now it didn't matter. She shivered under the spray for three minutes and was wide awake in five. Fighting a hint of a headache, she wrestled open her case and dragged on jeans.

'Crumpled, but you'll do,' she told them, adding an equally crumpled T-shirt. At least the flight had restored her faith in air travel. But, then, *this* journey had been planned. The last one hadn't been.

The brief trip for the funeral had been a nightmare. Fractured internal flights. Storms causing disruption across the USA. And a desperate ache of loss inside that had accompanied the unscheduled flight to England.

Tying up her work with her drug rehab patients had been essential. Abbie's concern was that their trust in her was preserved and so she had promised to return to them immediately after the funeral. Her one consolation had been the three months' leave she would take at a later date to clear up her father's affairs.

As she stood in her bedroom, Abbie's thoughts went back to the funeral. The tiny church, packed to its seams. Tilly village turning out *en masse*. And Caspar Darke's brooding presence beside her. Tall and broad-shouldered, with that shock of black hair and dark, dangerous eyes. Not a man to ignore, she had thought absently. Then had sunk grievingly back into oblivion.

Abbie shook her head a little as if to clear her mind. From her window she gazed up at the cloudless English sky. A few gulls circled, calling noisily as they dipped low, scavenging for food. Her soft green eyes followed their path downward, but when her gaze dropped to the hedge, so did her heart.

In the field next door a lorry was depositing gravel into a heap. Its hydraulics were working frantically under the strain. Abbie stared at what looked horribly like foundations.

Of what? A house?

No, too big. But whatever it was, it had no right to be there. Not in *her* field!

She flew out of the room and down the stairs. Where was he? Somewhere in the house—hiding, obviously.

'Cas is staying in the house,' Dad had written to tell her just after she'd moved to the States. 'Might as well have the room above yours, Abbie.'

Dream on, Dad. A total stranger living in the house? Well, a strange locum anyway. Dad might have trusted him, but she certainly didn't. Heck, he hadn't said two words to her before she'd left for the States. Ignored her practically. Yet he was living here. In the house. *Her* house.

She found him, eventually, in the surgery. 'What's happening out there?' she demanded, shocked to see him installed in Dad's chair behind the desk. 'Who are those people in the field?'

He put down his pen and stared up at her. Dark, unfathomable eyes that didn't blink once. 'Don't you know?'

'Know what? That's the practice land—*Dad's* land.'

'Not any longer. Your father sold it—twelve months ago.'

'That's ridiculous.' She laughed incredulously. 'Dad would never sell the practice land—never.'

'I'm afraid he did. To me.'

'You're joking—he would have told me,' she choked.

'No, it's the truth, Abbie.'

'This isn't funny,' she blurted, her eyes widening. 'Not in the least.'

'Abbie…obviously there are things we should talk about.'

'Lots of things, Dr Darke. Like the field for a start.'

'Cas,' he corrected. 'Call me Cas. I think we should be on first-name terms by now, don't you?'

'No, I don't.' Her cheeks flamed. 'We've barely ever spoken—'

'Because you've not been here to speak to,' he muttered, cutting her off sharply.

'I had to go back to the States,' she retorted, determined to defend herself. 'There wasn't a choice.'

'Ah, yes, the career.' He arched an ironic eyebrow. 'How's it going by the way?'

'Fine, thank you,' she snapped, ignoring the sarcasm. 'Now, about the field—'

'Abbie, I can't stop to discuss it now. I have a surgery to run.'

'Not for much longer,' Abbie retaliated. 'I'm home now. I don't know what your plans are...' She stopped, hoping he'd tell her, but he didn't. He just sat there, still with that damned eyebrow quirked. 'Well, anyway, that's something else we need to discuss,' she added feebly. 'Meantime, I'm going to look at my field.'

'*My* field, Abbie. And one more thing.' He smiled a smile that revealed the most perfectly white and even teeth she'd ever seen in her life.

'What?' she said, ignoring them.

'I intend to take surgery until the very last day that Tilly House Surgery is open—as your father intended.' He stared at her, his dark eyes pinning her. Eyes that were a deep, burnished brown but looked black.

'Well, we'll see about that,' she muttered, and stormed out. Who did he think he was, telling her what he was going to do?

The arrogance of the man. How dared he make such a threat?

The field was full of earthmoving vehicles and shouting workmen. She traipsed round it, too furious to talk, and simply glowered. How could Dad have sold the land? To anyone, let alone him?

This was where she'd kept her ponies, where she'd first learnt to ride. It was Tilly House land and always would be. Glancing disdainfully at a sign that announced a new development, she left the field in disgust.

The following morning, Abbie felt better. No headache. A light sleep. And even the noise next door didn't seem so threatening. Probably because it was only seven and they hadn't got started yet, she thought, glancing from the window. A few workmen were on site but not the lorries.

At least her body had settled down. Her tan was glowing and her hair was manageable. She dressed in shorts and sandals and sprayed on some perfume that reminded her of LA.

Downstairs she found the kitchen empty. The cupboards hadn't seen a lick of paint or polish in all the time she'd been away. And when, a few moments later, she stood in the hall, there was more evidence of neglect.

She hadn't noticed yesterday. She'd been too angry.

Sun stole weakly through the coloured panes of the front door and onto the faded wallpaper. Fabric lightshades hung limply, festooned in cobwebs.

'Oh, Dad, I miss you,' she sighed, shivering. 'I wanted to come home. Why didn't you let me?'

As if to spoil her moment of self-pity, the surgery door opened. Caspar appeared, dressed in a smooth blue shirt and dark trousers. Abbie glanced down at the powerful legs and narrow waist bound by a strip of polished leather. He raised his hand and drew it slowly through the thick black hair that ran lazily over his collar.

'I think we've unfinished business,' she said calmly, despite the contradictory lurch of her stomach.

'In here.' He shrugged. 'Or the kitchen.'

'The surgery will be fine.'

The door snapped closed behind her.

'You made certain claims yesterday—' she began, then stopped as he narrowed his eyes.

'Trusting little soul, aren't you?' He pulled out a chair and sat down. 'Obviously you're still of the same opinion. That I'm lying.'

Abbie smiled. Coldly. 'Why should I believe a stranger? We're hardly bosom pals.'

'It could have been different. Had you tried a bit harder.'

'Harder? Huh!' She folded her arms.

'You didn't like me two years ago and you still felt the same at your father's funeral.'

'I was upset,' she retaliated.

'I know, and I made allowances. I tried to talk to you, to explain. But all I got was that little-girl pout and silence. What was it, four...five hours that you had to suffer my company? You wouldn't even come back to the house.' He shook his head slowly. 'To be honest, I'm surprised you managed even that short time away from your schedule.'

Abbie took a breath. 'My...schedule, as you call it, is none of your business. I was lucky to get here at all. And you didn't make it any easier by looking so damned pleased when I told you I had to go straight back to the States.'

'No doubt it was an enforced return,' he replied sardonically.

'It was, actually. I had to arrange leave. For now.'

'And may I ask…how long it is this time? Four days, a week?'

'No,' she replied loftily, 'I've arranged a sabbatical.'

'A *sabbatical*,' he repeated slowly. 'My, my.' His eyes narrowed into suspicious chinks. 'And what exactly do you intend to do in the course of this…sabbatical?'

'Everything.' She sank into the nearest chair and folded her hands loosely in her lap. 'You may have ingratiated yourself with my father, *Caspar*. He was obviously too ill to recognise an opportunist when he saw one. But as far as I'm concerned, you'll have to give me proof that you own Dad's land. Incontestable, one hundred per cent proof.'

'A modest little request,' he muttered, and lifted the phone. 'But for a skilled opportunist, I think I can oblige.'

'What are you doing?'

'If it's proof you want, it's proof you'll have.' One long finger jabbed at the keypad and he handed her the phone. 'Gerard Store, your father's solicitor.'

Oh God, it's true, Abbie thought as she took the phone. He wasn't bluffing. She turned as far as she could in the chair to hide her humiliation. Five minutes later it was all over.

'Well, did you get your proof?'

She turned slowly and gritted her teeth. 'I don't know how you managed it but somehow you persuaded Dad into selling you his land.'

'Obviously I cast spells,' he said, and smiled.

'If there's a way to fight you,' she snarled, 'I'll find it. In fact, I think you should know that I intend to see Gerard tomorrow. I shall make every effort to take legal steps to reclaim that land.'

For a minute she thought she'd gone too far. Lightning glittered under the thick black lashes. The reclining, muscular frame tightened and he stood up, a rock of a man.

'In that case, you'll need the keys to your father's car.' He took them out of the drawer and dropped them on the desk in front of her. 'I've had it taxed and insured and the tank's full of petrol.'

Then, almost as though the control that he'd exerted was near to snapping, he clamped his jaw shut, strode past her and out of the surgery.

The thud of the door made her jump.

She closed her eyes and bit back tears. 'Why did you do it, Dad?' she whispered softly. 'Why did you sell our land? To *him*, of all people.'

* * *

'I'm afraid there is nothing I can do,' Gerard Store told her the following day. 'Your father left you the house and surgery and, of course, the trust fund. It was made up of the bulk of the money from the sale of the land.'

'When did Dad sell it?' she asked, her heart sinking by the minute.

'Your father completed the sale a year ago.'

'But why, Gerard? He bought the land with Mum when they first moved to Tilly thirty years ago.'

'I assumed it was to enable him to create the trust fund. He was concerned that it would be free of heavy penalties in the event of his death.'

'Was he ill then?' Abbie suggested. 'Is that why he did it?'

'Abbie, your father was getting on.' Gerard Store's tone was firm. 'I can't say if he was ill, since he didn't confide in me. But he was a sensible man and knew that it was only right to put his affairs in order.'

She made no further progress and left. 'At least the car's in working order,' Abbie murmured to herself as she drove through the village. She took comfort from its smell; old, worn leather and a whiff of oil bringing back bittersweet memories.

'Oh, Dad, it's such a muddle. Was it him? *That* man? What power did he have over you?'

Abbie glanced fondly at the cottages sprinkled along the streets. The quaint little shops and colourful market square. Her childhood had been spent here, amongst the community she knew so well. Friends, neighbours and patients of her father had become like a family after her Mum had died. At ten, she had learned to adjust to the vacant space in her life. The people of Tilly had taken Dr Scott's daughter to their hearts. And she loved them for it.

Then another thought struck her. What was it that Caspar Darke had said? Something about treating *his* patients until the very last day the surgery was open. 'As your father intended...' Yes, that was it. So what was it that Caspar had really meant?

She almost didn't see the lorry. It coasted round the bend and into the field. She braked and sat watching it.

What *exactly* was being built there? she wondered, then slapped the palm of her hand on her forehead. 'You idiot!' she groaned. 'Why didn't you ask Gerard?'

Flats, apartments, holiday homes? Tilly village was busier every season. Had Caspar recognised its potential? Decided to build some monstrosity there?

Barely able to wait until the lorry had reversed in, Abbie drove up to the house with a screech of brakes.

The dark blue four-wheel-drive wasn't there. Abbie grabbed her bag and hurried indoors to investigate, but all she found was a note on the desk. 'On visits. Mobile number below. Cas.'

She humphed and tossed the note in the bin. From the surgery window she could see the workmen's vehicles. The lorry, which had discharged its load, was about to exit the field.

'Well, I might as well look around,' she murmured, and narrowed her eyes at the desk. No appointment book. Pens, pencils and a dog-eared medical tome. Other than that, the surgery was just as her father had kept it. A tall cabinet on the right. The records carousel on the left. A comfortable easy chair for the patient. Wallpaper and paintwork sadly peeling.

What had been in Dad's mind before his death? she wondered as she twisted the carousel. Had he been thinking of selling the house and surgery, too?

It didn't make sense. He'd loved this place to distraction. It was home—*their* home. He wouldn't have left it. Would he?

Just then the telephone rang.

'May I speak to Dr Darke?' a woman's voice asked.

'He's not here at the moment.' Abbie paused. 'This is Dr Abbie Scott. Can I help?'

'Oh, Abbie, it's Josie here. Josie Dunning from the farm up the road. Sorry about your dad, love. Didn't stop to speak to you at the funeral last month. You looked pretty out of it.'

'I was a bit, Josie,' Abbie admitted. 'How can I help?'

'It's Susan. She's moaning about cramps again. I told her, it's all to do with the baby, like Dr Darke said. Called it some grand name he did but, to be honest, to my mind it's just being pregnant and you just have to put up with it.'

'You mean *your* Susan. Is she pregnant?'

'Over seven months gone, dear. You two went to the village school together, didn't you? Well, I'm sorry to say Susan fell in with a rum lot just after you left for America. Trouble is, he upped and left when she got pregnant and she's back at home with her pa and me now. Not that she's very happy about the situation and, frankly, neither is her dad.'

'I'll come myself, Josie. Can you cope till I get there?'

'I been coping with our Susan for the past twenty-nine years.' Josie chuckled. 'So a few more minutes won't harm.'

Abbie searched for and found her father's case. She packed the things she thought she would need and slipped Susan's records from the carousel.

Before leaving, she glanced into the tiny treatment room. It hadn't changed. Linen, towels and tissue and instruments were neatly placed on the trolley. The glaring difference was an array of colourful notes stuck to a corkboard above.

On her way out she bumped into a box. The appointment book was on top of it and she picked it up, turning the pages thoughtfully. Her father had marked very few. The majority of appointments were written in the same hand as those on the notes. Then, more recently, a careful instruction had been written in capitals across the top of the page.

OPEN SURGERIES FROM NOW ON.

The box beneath, was labelled Dr Caspar Darke. Abbie would have kicked it if it hadn't been a computer. And by the details on the invoice stuck to the side, it was a highly sophisticated one.

'So he plans to stay, does he?' Abbie straightened her back. 'We'll see about that.'

By the time she had reversed the car out of the drive, she had mentally given Caspar his marching orders, slung his belongings onto the front lawn and watched him drive off in a cloud of dust. It was a pleasing thought and she savoured it as she drove.

Her mood lifted instantly. It was a gorgeous day, she was home and going on her first call. It felt almost…almost…like her training year, when she had come to help Dad for a few months. Before America. If only she'd told Dad then that she wanted to stay…

If only she'd actually said how happy she was.

But she hadn't. And she'd gone off to America to please him.

Abbie listened to Susan Dunning's foetal heart-beat and smiled. As far as she could detect, Susan was healthy and so was Junior. However, Susan's abdominal discomfort and swollen legs were obviously adding to her distress.

'There's nothing to worry about, Sue.' Abbie recalled her friend's highly strung nature and spoke reassuringly. 'You've got polyhydramnios, a condition related to pregnancy. Hence the stomach cramps and swelling around your legs, but your records indicate that you've had your scan and all's well.'

'So it's a case of grin and bear it, is it?' Susan Dunning pushed her short dark hair from her face and frowned. A petulant face still, Abbie thought reflectively.

'We'll keep an eye on you. But the answer's rest. Have you been on your feet a lot?'

'She has,' interrupted Josie, coming into the room. She handed Abbie a cup of tea. 'Wanders around all day long. Says we haven't got satellite TV or a hi-fi and she's dying of boredom.'

'You're so old-fashioned, Mum,' Susan wailed. 'Everyone's got satellite these days.'

'Well, we haven't and that's that. Money doesn't grow on trees, my girl.'

'So you keep telling me,' Susan muttered, and Josie raised her eyes.

'Well, just another six weeks and the baby will keep you occupied,' Abbie said, changing the subject quickly.

Josie tutted and left the room. Abbie drank her tea and listened to Susan's catalogue of woe. Ralf, her man, had disappeared, along with the rent of their flat in Tilly village. Susan had been evicted.

'Men are selfish swine,' declared Susan as she lowered her feet to the ground. It was chilly in the farmhouse, even for May. A log fire crackled in the grate and Abbie cast a curious glance at her old friend.

'Why do you say that?' she asked.

'Well, aren't they? Dad never paid me any attention. He was too busy with the farm. And Ralf was off as soon as he found out about the baby. It was different for you. You had a lovely dad. Not like mine. More interested in cows than his own daughter.' Susan narrowed her eyes and sat forward. 'It was a shock, your dad going like he did. But at least you have that nice doctor to help you. Now, there's a man I could go for in a big way.'

Abbie spluttered into her tea, but Susan didn't notice. There was a glazed expression in her eyes. 'He's been lovely to me. Got me another scan and fixed up transport to the hospital. And those amazing eyes. They make me shiver, they do. He seems to look right into you…'

Abbie finished her tea quickly. 'I'll look in again next week.'

'What about Dr Darke? Will he be coming round?'

'I've no idea.' Abbie shrugged and picked up her case.

'Not married, then?' Susan asked as Abbie went to leave. 'No significant other?'

'No,' Abbie replied, and Susan gave a short laugh.

'Who'd have thought at school that neither of us would be married by our thirties? You always said you wanted to marry a doctor and live in the village. I always wanted to travel abroad and marry someone rich. Didn't work out quite that way for either of us, did it? I'm stuck at home and you've got that glamorous job in America, treating all those film stars.'

Abbie breathed a sigh of relief as Josie bustled in. 'You leaving, then, Abbie? I'll walk with you to the car.'

Outside the sun was shining and the farm was bathed in a heat haze. It was clear Josie wanted to speak without Susan hearing. Sounding breathless, she leaned wearily against the car.

'Are you feeling all right, Josie?' Abbie asked, but Josie waved her hand dismissively.

'Just a bit out of breath these days. But nothing a cup of tea and sit-down won't cure.' She took in a long breath and cleared her throat. 'What I wanted to say is, that your young man's been very good to our Susan.'

'You mean Dr Darke?'

Josie nodded. 'It was him who found her. God knows what would have happened if he hadn't.'

Abbie frowned. 'Found her? Where, Josie?'

'You don't know?' Josie raised her eyebrows and sighed. 'She went down to the cliffs when she found out—about the baby. Very unpredictable is our Susan, as you must remember from school. Anyway, he brought her back home and talked some sense into her.'

'You don't think Susan would have harmed herself?'

'She threatened it, the silly girl. Just to spite that good-for-nothing Ralf, if not to send us to an early grave. Five daughters we've had. Eight grandchildren. And our Susan has been more trouble than the lot put together.'

When Abbie left she thought about what Josie had said. Cas had, it seemed, averted a catastrophe. She was still thinking about it when she arrived at the surgery and parked. Leaning her arm on the window, she was deep in thought when a shadow fell across the car.

'Where have you been?' Cas's dark gaze bore down on her.

'To see Susan Dunning.' Abbie climbed out of the car. She felt at less of a disadvantage on two feet. 'Her mother rang.'

'Then why didn't you call me on the mobile?'

'No need.' She shrugged. 'I dealt with it.'

'Susan Dunning is my patient.' He sounded ruffled and she suppressed a smile. 'All you had to do was ring me.'

'Susan is an old friend. I've known the Dunnings for years.'

'I couldn't give a damn how long you've known them. In case of an emergency, I left you my mobile number.'

'It wasn't an emergency.' Abbie shrugged again. 'And even if it was—' Her voice was drowned by the sudden roar of an engine behind the hedge.

Cas grabbed her arm and propelled her towards the house.

'What exactly,' she demanded in the hall, 'is your problem?'

'You,' he growled, then pointed to the surgery. 'Now, go in there. Sit down and listen.'

CHAPTER TWO

'Now, let's get one thing straight.' Cas wagged a finger in her face. 'I wasn't your father's enemy. I was his friend. I admired him and if there is one thing I regret about all this, it's him not being here to tell you about the field himself.'

'I couldn't agree more,' Abbie said coldly. He'd had the cheek to push her down in the chair and treat her like a child. But she hadn't lost her voice. 'However, you seem to be making a pretty good job of talking for him.'

'I'm attempting to reason with you. I understand you're upset, but are you always this difficult?'

'Only when I arrive home and find a complete stranger practically taking over.'

'What was I supposed to do? Where have you been for the last two years?' He held up his hands before she could reply. 'Don't answer that,' he sighed, lifting his eyes wearily. 'I know the answer. Your glamorous *career*!'

'How dare you?' she spluttered, cricking her neck to look up at him. 'You know nothing about me.'

'I know enough,' he replied, narrowing his eyes and glaring. 'Absence speaks for itself in my book. And before you open that bolshie little mouth once more, watch my lips. I—am—not—leaving—here. Got it? I'm staying. Until my contract is up. Until I've done all that your father asked me to do.'

'Which is exactly what?' she flung at him defiantly.

He laughed, but his laughter was empty. 'To look after you, sadly.'

She stared at him, a sudden vision of him hovering over her like a great dark cloud exploding thunder every time she moved. 'That's ridiculous.'

'At least we agree on something.'

'I don't need your help.'

He laughed loudly this time. 'Without doubt.'

'So—so—go!' She stood up, vowing to hit him if he touched her. But he didn't. Instead, he went to the window and stared out, his shoulders sagging. 'I wish I could.'

'Then what's stopping you?' She moved cautiously around the desk to peer at him.

'My word. I gave it to your father. And I can't let him down.'

That, she had to admit, was probably the one remark—or two—that she didn't have an answer for. 'That's not fair,' she whimpered, and sat down again. 'It really isn't.'

He turned slowly and leaned his back against the wall. 'No, I agree, it isn't. On either of us.'

'How long have you got left on your contract?' She really didn't want to know the answer.

'Three months.'

'Great.'

'Isn't it?'

'If you stay here, you won't have much time for your precious project.' She still wasn't giving up.

He eyed her warily. 'So you've spoken to Gerard. And what did he tell you?'

'Nothing. Practically.'

'Nothing?' The hollowed cheekbones drew in. 'Well, let me enlighten you. I'm building a health centre. A polyclinic.'

She stared at him. 'A *what*?'

'A polyclinic. A centre that caters for traditional and complementary therapies.'

She blinked. 'And Dad knew about it? This…this *polyclinic*?'

'Your father was as enthusiastic as I was.' He peeled himself away from the wall and sat down, drawing his hand slowly over his jaw. 'I wrote an article in a medical journal. Your father read it and phoned me. We met, he asked me to locum at Tilly House and familiarise myself with the location. The rest is history.'

'But…but what about the surgery?' she demanded. 'A health centre would make this place redundant.'

'Abbie, look around you. We're already redundant.'

'We still have some patients,' she argued stubbornly. 'It's not as if we're totally unworkable.'

'Yes, we do,' he agreed. 'But we haven't taken anyone on since you left. Many have transferred to the next village or the towns. That's why we hold open surgeries, so that people can come whenever they like. It's a privilege I think they deserve.' He inhaled slowly. 'Abbie, your father was a man of vision. He accepted the surgery had come to a natural end.'

'Tilly House was his life,' Abbie protested. 'And Mum's.'

'*Was*,' Cas repeated with emphasis. 'Health provision has changed beyond recognition. This place just isn't up to it. Your father saw that. He shared my views on medicine and agreed that a polyclinic would be the way forward.'

Abbie felt as if they were discussing a stranger. As if she'd never really known her own father. If what this man said was true, why hadn't she known of her father's unfulfilled dreams?

'I'm sorry,' Cas said softly, and she found herself being drawn against the hard, comforting chest. A tear squeezed under her eyelids and to hide the others she let her head rest there.

Ten minutes ago she'd wanted to hit him, now she didn't know what she wanted. Yes, she did. She wanted this, his hands on her back and playing in her hair and the wild and wonderful feeling that accompanied it. She was sorry for herself and she knew it. She didn't deserve the comforting. But she didn't want him to stop either.

He held her away gently, quirking an eyebrow. 'Green eyes. Green as a cat's, but rounder, prettier,' he decided, 'with little yellow flecks. Lovely eyes.'

'I don't feel lovely,' she mumbled. 'I feel—'

'Angry?'

'No.' The eyebrow lifted a fraction and she sighed. 'Well, yes. Angry that I seem to be ignorant of so much.'

'You're tired,' he told her. 'You haven't had time to adjust. Come in the other room and I'll light a fire.'

She nodded but given the choice, she would have stayed where she was. She would just like to *be* here, having him touch her this way...tender, comforting touches that flicked

over her skin and hair and made her feel ridiculously happy.

Despite the sun on the window-pane, it was
ridiculously cold in the house. Cas pushed her
gently down on the sofa and she watched him
kneel by the grate. Same floral carpet, same tatty
mat, she thought sadly, with a big threadbare
patch that had got bigger and bigger over the
years.

Cas was right. The house was redundant.

'I'm all right now.' Abbie sat on the edge of
the sofa.

'Do as you're told and rest.' He lifted her legs
and dropped them on the cushions. The skirt of
her dark blue suit crept up, the one she had worn
this morning to see Gerard. Catching his glance,
she urged it down and gave another sniff of disgust. Mostly at herself for being so weak.

He took off her shoes and threw them aside
and she shifted uneasily, feeling self-conscious.
She wriggled, adjusting the hem of her skirt
again.

'Lean forward.' He dragged a pillow off the
easy chair and propped it behind her. She smelt
his aftershave, clearer this time because their
bodies were close. Whatever it was, she had the
smell mentally tagged, Caspar.

She tilted her head, avoiding the long arm covered in blue linen. Her eyes skimmed the broad back as he pummelled the cushion, then dropped to his thighs. She swallowed, her gaze lingering on the magnificent muscles.

Dark eyes met hers as she looked up. 'Tea?'

'Mmm, please.' Her colour rose. 'One sugar.'

Why was he being so nice to her? she wondered when she was on her own. She should really go for a walk, blow the cobwebs away. Take the cliff path, find a deserted cove and watch the surf. Only she didn't really want to.

She wanted to stay here. And talk. And be with him.

Sighing, she gazed round the room that hadn't changed in her lifetime. Long sash windows framed by heavy curtains. Photos of her at school on the walls. One of her mother on the mantelpiece. A family collage on the sideboard. A glass case full of china, a nest of tables, one with a broken leg. She saw her father wrestling with it, spilling his tea and changing tack to the big easy chair instead.

Cas appeared, juggling mugs in one hand. He put them on the coffee-table and sat on the sofa. 'When did you last eat?'

'Breakfast, I think.'

'It's nearly five.'

Abbie shrugged. 'I'll have something later on.'

'You don't need me to tell you—'

'No, I don't.' She nodded. 'I'll eat. Promise.'

They sat quietly, sipping tea. Her toes had somehow reached his thigh. It was a warm, firm thigh that made her shiver inside. There wasn't much about him that wasn't firm, she decided, trying not to let him see what she was doing. And she couldn't help doing it. Watching him, studying the way he moved, turned his head, thrust back the hair that perpetually fell over his brow.

'Do you want to talk?' he asked, and she pulled back her gaze, meeting his eyes and hoping he wasn't doing his trick. Reading her thoughts.

'About Dad?'

'About anything. So long as we don't fight. At least until we've finished our tea.'

She hid a smile. 'How long had Dad been ill?'

'How much did you know when you left for the States?'

Abbie shook her head. 'Nothing at all. He didn't tell me he was ill—ever. I would never have gone if I'd realised.'

For a moment he stared at her, then put his mug on the table. He sat back, his fingers weaving absently around her toes. 'If I hadn't seen it for myself he wouldn't have told me. It was just a quick attack. But I happened to be around—and then the cat was out of the bag.'

'Angina, you mean?'

He nodded. 'I made him go for tests. He refused at first. Said it was nothing, not enough exercise, indigestion…all the old excuses. Finally, I insisted.'

'And?' The pain of hearing what her father had gone through was softened by Cas's touch. She realised he wasn't conscious of his fingers on her feet. Softly rubbing, pressing and soothing. She swallowed hard. And prayed he wouldn't stop.

'He needed a bypass. Sooner rather than later.'

'Was he…was he down to have one?'

He nodded absently. As though he were there in that small space of time that had eluded her. 'Yes…last year. Terry Maguire, St Catherine's top cardiologist took him over. Lined him up for October.'

'But Dad never had it?' she pressed.

'He got flu. Was pretty groggy for a couple of months. An op was out of the question unfortunately.'

Abbie recalled the letter and nodded. 'That's right. I remember. He wrote to me about the flu. I wanted to come home for Christmas but he told me not to. Said I should leave it to the New Year when the bug had gone.'

'Well, then,' Cas said quietly, turning to her, 'there's your answer. I guess he was buying himself time.'

'Time for what?' she mumbled thickly. 'I wanted to come home. Was desperate to see him. I could have done something—anything.' There was a hitch in her voice and she bit her lip. She wasn't going to get upset again. Not in front of Cas. But her lip quivered and he saw it.

'Abbie…?'

'I'm OK.' She nodded, her head bowed. He let go of her feet, lifted her legs and swivelled along the sofa. Carefully, as though she might protest, he unravelled her clenched fingers and drew her against him.

She trapped the sigh in her throat. 'It's…it's all right. I'm not going to cry.'

'You should if you want.' She buried her head against his shirt and he stroked her hair.

She didn't know which she liked best, her hair or her feet being touched. She didn't know anything any more. She didn't seem to have a mind, just pleasure zones that burst into life when he touched her. And she felt even guiltier, because he was probably feeling sorry for her.

'I really am OK,' she said, but hung onto him all the same. It felt safe and secure, laying her head just beneath his chin. She could feel the rhythm of his heart. A strong heart, beating regularly and so soothing.

'Your father was an independent man, Abbie,' he murmured above her. 'Too much so at times.'

'Is that why he distanced me?'

'It was his way of doing things.' He added softly as he stroked her hair, 'He had his reasons.'

'I s'pose.' Exhaustion crept into her bones like a warm tide. Her lids felt heavy as she struggled against sleep. It felt so good in his arms. She wanted to lift her face, to look into his eyes, but she didn't have the strength.

Her dreams were of Cas, of brooding brown eyes and thick, ebony hair. He was walking away down the lane toward the field. She was calling him, running in her bare feet.

And suddenly he turned…

She slept peacefully and, for the first time in weeks, without interruption.

It was Friday and she was home.

This time Abbie woke knowing where she was. Cas had put her to bed and she'd slept all night. She felt almost afraid to disturb the composure that rest had brought.

Showering was bliss, her body craving the water. Dressing took a few moments—fresh lacy white underwear, summer trousers and a white T-shirt and comfortable white pumps. And a new day.

She found him in the kitchen, his back turned to her. A crisp white short-sleeved shirt and a pair of light-coloured trousers made him look even taller. Just as in her dream, his dark hair curled over his collar.

He was making coffee and she inhaled. 'That smells good.'

He turned and for a brief second frowned. Then when he saw her smiling he grinned. 'You look better.'

She tilted her head, her hair still damp from showering. 'Just better—or much better?'

'Whichever one will incriminate me the least.'

She raised her eyebrows. 'I suppose I asked for that.'

His grin widened. 'Coffee?'

'A barrelful, please.'

He turned back to the coffee-pot. 'I take it you slept well.'

'Very well.' She pulled out a chair and sat down. 'Cas?' she asked softly.

He stiffened for a second, then turned. 'What?'

She smiled. 'It's not a complaint. It's a thank you. For last night. For looking after me.'

'You remember?' He looked guarded.

'I remember complaining you shouldn't be taking off my clothes when you put me to bed. You said you'd seen it all a thousand times before. At the time, I felt too sleepy to be insulted.'

He laughed. 'Actually, I *helped* you off with your blouse. You did the skirt.'

'You could have left me to freeze on the sofa all night.'

'I considered it.' One dark eyebrow quirked up. He sank down on a chair opposite her. 'Anyway, what are friends for?'

'Are we friends?' she asked cautiously.

'It would seem that way.' He eyed her darkly. 'And next door? How does stealing your land sit this morning?'

Abbie stiffened. 'I don't know. I haven't got that far yet.'

'Let me know the outcome.' He looked at her under thick black lashes. 'What are we going to do about surgeries?' He gulped back the coffee.

'What was the arrangement you had with Dad?'

He stretched out his long legs and sighed. 'In the early days, we shared them. When he was ill, there was no pattern. If he felt he could, he'd go out on a call or take surgery.'

'I gather you're not going to object to me doing the same? I mean, sharing surgeries and calls?'

'I can't stop you. This is your practice.' He stood up and pushed back his chair. 'Take the calls if you want. Go through the books. Do whatever you like.'

She had hoped for a moment they had come to a truce. But as she looked up at him, his dark eyes were mistrustful.

'Do you have a receptionist or someone to come in whilst you're out?' she asked hesitantly.

'We had a couple. Part-timers. The last one left to have a baby. Roughly about when your father died. I haven't bothered since. I've been meaning to. But I just haven't had the chance.' He looked at the clock on the wall. 'Better go. I've surgery at nine. Take Monday's if you like. I'll do the calls.'

'Great.' Abbie stood up. 'See you later.'

'You might. Then you might not. I usually eat out at the pub. I only shop once a month.'

She felt a flip of disappointment. 'OK. Well, see you when I see you.'

He cast her a frown, then nodded. She watched him go and wondered what he was really think-

ing. Well, she wasn't going to let her guard
down. Probably he wasn't either. But at least on
the surface, things had improved.

She could handle that.

Just.

Abbie didn't see Cas that night. And the next day
she got up early but he was gone. It was Saturday
and there didn't appear to be surgery. She should
have asked him if he had one at weekends.
Obviously not today.

The phone rang and she answered it.

'This is Howard Bailey,' a voice said, and
Abbie smiled.

'Mr Bailey, this is Abbie. Dr Scott's daughter.'

'Good grief, where did you spring from, lass?
Aren't you working in America, hobnobbing
with all them rich folk?'

Abbie paused before she answered. 'I'm home
for a while. Sorting out Dad's practice.'

'Eh, I was so sorry to hear about your dad,
Abbie. Knew him and your mother for years.'

'When was the last time you saw him?' Abbie
asked curiously.

'About two months back. Wasn't feeling too
good himself then but he came out to visit me
specially. We had a lot in common, what with
me having that heart valve put in. I had my first

valve four years ago but it started to play up and I had to have a replacement last year.'

'How are you now?' Abbie asked, listening to his slightly breathy tone.

'I'm feeling a bit shabby, to be honest.'

'Would you like me to come and see you?' Abbie asked hesitantly, remembering that she had agreed to discuss the visits and surgeries with Caspar.

'Now, that's an offer I can't refuse.' Howard chuckled. 'You know where I am. Over the grocer's in the village. I'll put the kettle on.'

Abbie replaced the phone as she sat at the office desk. Maybe she should have given Howard the choice of seeing either her or Cas. The alternative was to phone Cas on his mobile. She pulled out the waste-paper bin under the desk, but it was empty. Failing to find the note there, she rummaged through the appointment book.

Nothing.

Well, that was that. But Howard seemed happy to see her and she could probably find out from him just how her father had been on his last visit. Taking her father's case and Howard's notes, she drove to the village.

It was a hot May day and the market square was already busy. Sad that the cattle market had disappeared, Abbie thought wistfully as she parked by the greengrocer's. But the antiques market, which was really junk and bric-à-brac, was colourful enough. And she made a note to wander round it later.

Abbie waved at George Lambert, the grocer, who was also the baker. His two strapping sons ran the bakery at the back of the shop. The freshly made bread and cakes were advertised on the striped awning above.

Abbie slipped through the arched alleyway and into the bakery courtyard. The aroma of freshly baked bread was stunning. Howard Bailey, much heavier than she remembered him, was standing at the top of a wrought-iron stairway.

He led her into his flat, slightly out of breath, and sank down into a chair beside the window. 'Sit yourself down, lass,' he told her, bringing out a large handkerchief and mopping his brow. 'Kettle's boiling.'

In the end it was Abbie who made the tea and joined Howard at the table in the window.

'When did you have your heart-valve replacement?' Abbie studied the notes.

'Last year,' Howard told her breathlessly.

'And you've had your check-ups?'

'Most of them. I have to admit I missed the last two.'

Abbie looked up and frowned. 'Why?'

For a moment Howard bit his bottom lip, then slowly stroked back his mop of iron grey hair. He placed his hand on his stomach and patted the generous curve. 'Do you want the truth or am I allowed to fib?'

Abbie smiled, her green eyes twinkling. 'Has it anything to do with the shop below?'

Howard laughed loudly. 'You really are your father's daughter. He never missed a trick and neither do you. He only had to take one look at me when he came and he tore me off a strip. It's that wretched bread. Ever since they started baking downstairs, I simply can't resist it. It's torture, smelling it. If Ivy was alive she'd keep me in check, but I'm hopeless on my own.'

Abbie smiled gently. 'Have you put on weight since the op?'

Howard looked guilty. 'Over a stone. And it's still going on. I can't stop myself eating the stuff. After all, I don't drink or smoke. What other pleasure in life have I got and it's right on my doorstep? I was telling your Dr Darke last time I asked him for my anticoagulants. You know what he said?'

'No,' Abbie answered warily. 'What?'

'That if I ate enough of the right stuff I wouldn't feel hungry. He was going to write me out a list, but I didn't like the sound of that. So it was a bit of a relief, hearing your voice this morning.'

Abbie raised her eyebrows and sat forward, leaning her arms on the dining table. 'If you're still gaining weight, no wonder you're breathless.'

'That's what your dad said.'

'I'm going to sort you out a fresh appointment.'

Howard looked dismayed. 'They only put me on the scales and I get a lecture. Can't you give me something to stop me eating?'

'No, I can't. You need to see your consultant.'

'That's what your father said,' Howard admitted. 'And the young fellow.'

'Then all three of us must be right, mustn't we?'

Howard grinned. 'Yes, but you're prettier.'

Abbie smiled, then said slowly, 'Was Dad well when you saw him?'

'He did a good job of hiding his worries,' Howard replied quietly. 'It was the young one who made him have those medical tests.'

'You mean Dr Darke?'

'He looked after your dad like his own. Had a rough time in Tilly he did, when he first came. The locals only wanted to see your dad and not the rookie. Gave the chap the cold shoulder for a while.'

'Why was that?' Abbie asked curiously.

'Well, you know how tongues wag. That high falutin girlfriend of his came down from London. She upset one or two in the village, parking her posh motorcar in the middle of the road so Bob Armitage couldn't get his horsebox through, nor could the farrier. Then saying to Mrs Braidy in the chemist how a few things needed changing round here, that small shops was a thing of the past. She upset the poor old biddy good and proper.'

Abbie felt disturbed at this new revelation. Caspar had a girlfriend—so what? The fact that she seemed to have set Tilly village alight with gossip should be the least of her worries.

But it did worry her.

All the way back to the surgery. And continued to do so as she sat outside the surgery, staring at the four-wheel-drive parked by the garage.

CHAPTER THREE

CASPAR was standing in the surgery, leafing through the files in the cabinet that, as yet, Abbie hadn't explored. She knew they contained records of all the patients of Tilly House. Single-leafed folders with the appropriate information from health authorities. Since he couldn't have heard her come in, she stood in the open doorway and waited for him to turn.

In the moments her gaze lingered on him, she noticed how, when he moved, the arch of his shoulder blade emphasised the length of his back, which tapered down deliciously to a narrow waist. He had the hips and legs of an athlete. Initially she had only registered his height. But it was more than that. It was the way he was carved out. Solidly. Like a sculpture.

Her gaze lingered, drawn again to the thick, black hair that looked so luxurious. So smooth. And that wild inch curling over his collar, asking to be caressed…

Abbie came back from her thoughts as he turned. As if he had known she was watching him.

The dark eyes met hers with amusement. Their lids gave him an almost dreamy expression but Abbie was not deceived.

'Ah, the wanderer returns,' he murmured, thrusting the drawer closed.

'You weren't here when I came down this morning. I assumed you were out on calls.'

'Such as they were.'

'No surgery on Saturdays?' she queried.

'Once a month.' He shrugged and gestured to the chairs. 'Take your pick. They're both yours,' he added dryly.

Abbie sat down on the one beside the desk in order not to have to squeeze in between him and the cabinet.

He gave an imperceptible shrug as he lifted a pile of records from the top of the cabinet.

'Are those the patients you saw this morning?' she asked curiously.

'Three in all,' he said. 'A child with tonsillitis, someone with a torn ligament—and Susan Dunning.'

'Susan?' Abbie repeated, sitting up in the chair quickly. 'What's wrong?'

'Nothing. In fact, she's in the peak of health. Josie yielded to the devil and got a satellite dish. Susan hasn't stirred since.' He grinned and pearl white teeth flashed momentarily. 'Josie rang to let us know early this morning, saying we were welcome to celebrate the occasion with a cup of tea.'

'*We?*' Abbie queried.

'You were still sleeping.' He lifted his palms upward in a casual gesture. 'You needed the rest, so I didn't wake you.'

'But I would have preferred it if you—'

'So, shall we sort out what exactly we're going to do?' he interrupted, leaning back in his chair and frowning.

Abbie bit her lip, annoyed at not being told of Josie's message. 'Let's do as you suggested. Share everything. The surgeries, the calls and the weekend duty.'

'So you really are staying?' His frown deepened.

'I've got a month. At least, three weeks left of it.'

'Brilliant.' He was unable to hide the note of sarcasm in his voice. 'But what's the point?'

'The point is,' she replied without flinching, 'redundant as the surgery may be when this…this…what is it?'

'Polyclinic.'

'When this *polyclinic* of yours gets off the ground, I still have to decide what to do with this place. Presumably the patients of Tilly House will transfer to you?'

He nodded slowly. 'That's the general idea.'

'And Dad had no objections?' she queried again.

'I told you. Your father and I shared fundamental beliefs about the future of medicine. The polyclinic will comprise both. Traditional and complementary. And if your father had expressed a desire to partner me, I would have jumped at the chance.'

'But he didn't?' she persisted.

'Partnership wasn't an issue,' he answered shortly. 'Not with his illness.'

'But he sold you the land nevertheless?'

He nodded slowly. 'I admit that if your father hadn't, I would have been forced to look elsewhere. Securing the right environment and permission from the authorities was essential.'

'For you,' she added coolly. 'It was your brainchild. Not Dad's.'

'Initially, yes.' His dark eyes met hers calmly. 'But by the time your father died, it was as important to him as it is to me. We were both totally committed.'

Abbie sank back in her chair and nodded slowly.

'Obviously my word's still not enough,' he muttered, a dark eyebrow thrusting up. 'Why is it so hard for you to believe me, Abbie?' he asked incredulously. 'I'm not lying to you and never have.'

At that moment the telephone rang and Abbie watched him reach out to answer it. Perhaps because she was still deep in thought over his last remark, she wasn't aware of the expression slowly filling his face.

The telephone went down with a bang. 'That was Howard Bailey. Why the heck didn't you say you'd been to see him?'

'I was going to,' she began, 'only we got talking—'

'About you—again,' he yelled at her. 'And how you can't get it into that head of yours that I'm not out to damn well cheat you.'

Abbie rose to her feet. 'That's not true,' she breathed, her voice shaking. 'How dare you talk to me like that?'

'And how dare you interfere in the treatment of my patient?' he replied, standing up and glowering. 'It's taken me weeks to persuade Howard to agree to lose weight. Now he's telling me he's putting it off again until he's seen his consultant.'

'He's missed two appointment already,' Abbie said furiously. 'It's essential he attends.'

'Don't you think I don't know that? But what good will it achieve if he's puffing like a rhino the moment he steps on the scales? The man needs to reduce before he goes, not after!'

For one moment Abbie was speechless. 'I...I wasn't aware that—'

'No, you're aware of very little about other people, Abbie,' he broke in, his eyes glittering. 'Are you really so self-absorbed you can't see that I have Howard's best interests at heart? And, indeed, that of every other patient on your father's list? I'm not out to sabotage your precious little pedestal of stardom, and I couldn't give a damn what you think of me. Or, indeed, what you believe or don't believe.' He pulled back his shoulders and inclined his head. 'Hell, no wonder your father refused to involve you here. I dread to think what his life would have been like if he had.'

The last comment was like a physical blow. She reached out to steady herself on the desk. 'Get out,' she snarled. 'Out of *my* surgery!'

His lips curled into a twist of disdain. 'My *pleasure*,' he said with feeling, then strode to the door and slammed it behind him.

Half an hour later, Abbie was still sitting in the surgery, in the chair behind the desk this time, staring sightlessly at the appointment book in front of her.

She had been trying to examine it while reconciling her rage with the illogical guilt she felt over Howard Bailey. There had been nothing written on Howard's records to suggest that she shouldn't refer him to the consultant again. She wasn't a mind-reader. And most doctors would have whisked Howard promptly back to the hospital.

Nevertheless, Abbie found herself wishing she had followed her instincts and waited before visiting Howard.

However, the truth of the matter was that she was hurt—desperately hurt. Not by Cas's criticism of her work, but by his personal slant. What right had he to comment on her relationship with her father?

Abbie tried to relax as she heard him coming down the stairs. Her small, slender-boned fingers tapped the desk and she took a breath, waiting for him to enter.

Would she accept an apology?

Had he meant what he'd said about Dad not wanting to involve her in surgery affairs? Had Dad ever said anything to him that might suggest that?

She stiffened her back and waited. No, an apology wasn't going to wash. She would quietly but firmly tell him that they weren't suited to working together. She had decided to end the contract. He could fight it out legally if he wanted, but she couldn't accept his attitude...

Wouldn't accept it.

Abbie heard the front door open and a loud bang. What was he doing? She went to the window. Cas was pushing a suitcase into the back of the four-wheel-drive. She rushed to the door and yanked it open.

He collided with her in the hall. 'Here's the key to my room...sorry, *your* room.' He dropped it noisily on the hall table.

'You're going?' she said, and stared at the sports bag slung over his shoulder. 'Now?'

'Good guess,' he growled, and nodded to the stairs. 'There's a bureau of mine and a chest of drawers upstairs. You're welcome to them.'

'But...but what about your post...a forwarding address...?' she gabbled, following him outside.

'Shove the post over the hedge. Any of the guys will take it,' he muttered, flinging the sports bag into the open vehicle.

It was beginning to rain and she watched him shut the back door, running his hand through his hair, which looked blacker and wilder than ever. Then he glanced at her and stood for a moment.

'Cas...' she began, but he muttered and glared at her. Then he jumped in the car, revved loudly and disappeared down the drive in a cloud of dust.

Going on tiptoe, she craned her head. A glimpse of the blue metal roof sparkled wetly as the vehicle turned into the field.

He was going to live next door? In the field?

Abbie ran indoors and leapt the stairs two at a time. From her bedroom window she watched him park the car outside the portable unit on the field. Broad, hunched shoulders emerged and the back went up. A second or two later the door of the unit opened and he was thrusting his luggage inside. Then the door slammed shut.

Abbie stared at the cabin and the field, deluged in rain. At the green grass and brown earth of the four acres of farrow field that were turning into a quagmire before her eyes.

Cas had gone. *Really* gone.

She had told him to get out and he had. As simple as that.

She should be overjoyed.

Was overjoyed—of course.

She sat on the bed and looked around. The house was starting to feel like home again. The dratted man had gone and she could do what she wanted now—on her own terms without any interference at all.

Then she remembered the other night and the way he had held her and touched her, the feel of his fingers in her hair and the need that had filled her.

It was a need she still felt, deep inside her. A yearning, an ache, which she had squashed and pummelled into a place that she wasn't prepared to acknowledge. Somewhere deep and dark and unlockable. Because she didn't trust him. Because she was too proud to admit she had been wrong.

The phone seemed to know Cas had gone.

It rang day and night for the following week. Abbie took four morning surgeries, as was indicated in the book, and made her calls in the afternoon. Most people called her mobile if they couldn't reach her at home.

Most people wanted Caspar.

By the end of the week, she was exhausted and cold. Exhausted by broken sleep. Cold because the oil-fired boiler had ceased to function—again. Added to which she had been forced to listen to the praises of the departed locum.

'When will he be back?' was the question she hated most.

'I'm not sure,' she'd reply. And bite her lip.

'Salt of the earth' was her second least favourite.

'Yes, so I'm frequently told.'

On Friday, Abbie's surgery lasted until lunchtime—an uneventful morning of throat infections, hay fever and arthritis, an hour of signing prescriptions.

So different from her work in the States, she thought, her pen poised wearily as her mind flew back to the prescriptions that were carefully monitored by the drug rehabilitation centre she worked for.

The tragic cases had broken her heart—at first. Kids hooked on drugs at eight and nine. Men and women unable to retreat from a life of drug abuse. Babies, drug dependent from birth.

'Working with these people is awesome, you'll have to toughen up,' she had been advised. 'Don't have any expectations, Abbie. Don't judge. All you can do is treat the physical side— and listen.'

Dr Jon Kirk, her chief, had been right. The work had been awesome. Underpaid, endless hours and often frightening. She'd been initiated the hard way. A young mother and her child on heroin, bruised and battered by a violent partner. Abbie had, as Jon had told her, treated their wounds. There were others to help heal the emotional scars, amongst them, the founder of the rehab unit himself, Jon Kirk.

Abbie lowered her head into her hands and sighed. The last eighteen months had been tough. A revelation in human behaviour. But she had succeeded and in some small way helped those who hadn't been able to help themselves.

If only she had been able to tell Dad. Explain.

But how could she have disappointed him? How could she have told him the job he'd secured for her at a wealthy and prestigious private hospital had just not been for her? Cosmetic and often irrelevant surgery left her cold. She needed a challenge. A meaning to her life.

And drug rehabilitation had given it to her. Telling Dad about her change of course had been the hardest task. She'd put it off, intending to come home and break the news.

She'd kept her secret. And Dad had kept his, too.

And all she'd ever wanted had been Tilly House. To qualify, travel a little, then settle down and work. Here. Amongst the community she knew.

A screech of brakes in the distance brought Abbie upright in the chair. Her body tensed as she waited for the impact. It came, a sickening series of thuds followed by the sound of twisting, ripping metal. Then an eerie silence that had Abbie reaching for the phone and dialling the emergency services.

Grabbing her case, she hurtled from the surgery. In the lane a group of workmen joined her.

'I'm a doctor,' she told them breathlessly. 'What's happened?'

'It came from up there, on the bend,' a man in a reflective jacket told her, and they began to run. As they turned the corner, they found pieces of metal strewn across their path. With a lurch of her stomach, Abbie saw a figure in the road.

For a moment she couldn't catch her breath. Her eyes flickered over a long male body lying on its side. His arm seemed to be trapped in the upturned van. On the other side of the vehicle was a red car, its bonnet embedded in the van. She ran, her heart thumping, towards them.

'It's one of Benson's Dairies' vans,' someone yelled. 'Must've been on a delivery.'

Splinters of glass whipped across Abbie's legs and she realised she was running over shattered glass. Coming to a halt at the motionless figure on the ground, she felt a wave of nausea flow over her.

A long, naked back leanly compacted with muscle. Jeans covered in mud over long, powerful legs—and thick black hair curling over a tanned neck. Hair that she would have known anywhere.

'Cas!' she heard herself yelling as she fell to her knees.

'Watch out for the glass,' someone shouted. They tried to draw her back, but she pulled free.

'Cas! Cas!' She laid her hand tentatively on his shoulder. Her heart was beating so rapidly she could barely breathe. Leaning over him, she saw a pool of blood on the tarmac. 'Oh, God, no,' she whispered.

'I'm all right, Abbie,' he muttered, and looked up at her, barely daring to move his head. His right arm was burrowed into a jagged hole which was all that remained of the window.

'Thank God,' she breathed. 'What happened, Cas?'

'I was in the lane…mending the fence. They were travelling in opposite directions. God knows what happened…it was a head-on collision. The guy in here's unconscious—and there's a woman in the car on the other side. Had to leave her,' he faltered, lifting his free hand to steady himself against the crumpled metal. 'Don't think she's hurt badly...told her to stay where she was...'

'And the driver of this?' Abbie asked, staring at the impossibly twisted metal.

'He's trapped...unconscious...that's all I know.' Beads of sweat were standing out over his face as he spoke. 'I saw the blood...reached in...found his arm and felt a pulse. I'm elevating it. Can feel a rip in his wrist. Can't let go. Just managed to...to drag my shirt over the wound...'

'Tell me how I can help.' Abbie tried to lean down to see into the hole that Cas had forced his arm through.

'Are the emergency services coming?'

'Soon.'

'Then give me something more to help staunch the blood.' His face was strained with effort.

There was nothing to offer but her clothes and Abbie undid the buttons of her blouse, grateful for the flimsy covering of her slip.

'Damn it,' Cas cursed as he tried to thread it through the hole with his free hand. 'The angle's impossible.'

Abbie looked up at the crowd of workmen. 'Can someone lay a coat down over the glass?'

One of them removed his reflective jacket and Abbie squatted down on it, leaning gently over

Cas's body. She took the blouse and reached towards the hole.

'Go slowly,' he warned her. 'If you reach my fingers, try to thread the cloth around them. There's no way I can release the pressure.'

She worked blindly, terrified of disturbing his grip. It was all she could do not to visualise what was inside the van and she had to force herself to stay calm. Eventually she managed to plug whatever spaces she found, biting her lip to keep focused.

'That's helped,' he whispered, and she felt his free arm come over to brush her face supportively. 'Keep your hand where it is, if you can.'

She nodded, exerting all her strength. Cas was right, the angle was impossible and she was straining every muscle. Finally she closed her eyes then suppressed a sigh of relief as she heard sirens.

'They're here,' Cas murmured, and she nodded.

'Thank God,' she whispered, praying for a miracle.

The twisted mountain of metal shook, despite the measures taken by the fire crew to steady it. It was a painstaking procedure that seemed to last hours rather than moments. When a cheer went up from the workmen on the far side, Abbie let out a soft sigh.

'They've found him,' Cas murmured, and Abbie felt him release his grip. 'Take your arm out slowly,' he warned her. 'I won't move until you're free.'

She did so, withdrawing through the hole and easing back her shoulder. Afterwards, he did the same.

'Are you hurt?' he asked as they sat up.

'No…just…' She looked down at her hands. 'Messy.'

He nodded wearily, stretching out to flex the muscles of his arm. 'Me, too. Let's find somewhere to clean up.'

One of the workmen had bottled water and they used it to wash with. Cas frowned at her afterwards. 'You're shaking,' he murmured, and drew her against him.

'I'm OK. Just stiff—and a little cramped.'

For a moment he held her gaze. 'Thanks, Abbie.'

'For what?'

'For being there.' His dark eyes held hers and she smiled.

'I didn't do much. *Couldn't* do much…'

'It was enough,' he replied quietly, squeezing her arm gently. 'If you're OK I'll see if I can help.'

She nodded. 'I'm here if you want me.'

He paused before he left her, quirking up an eyebrow. 'Remember you said that, Abbie Scott.'

After he had gone, a kind soul draped a blanket round her shoulders and she finally stopped shaking.

'I've a flask in the car,' a young policewoman told her, and Abbie smiled gratefully. They sat together on the back seat and Abbie sipped the tea. 'What happened to the girl?' she asked, suddenly realising she hadn't seen her.

'We drove her to hospital. Bruises and shock mostly,' the WPC explained. 'She was lucky— at least, luckier than the driver of the van. Does he stand a chance, do you think?'

Abbie shrugged. 'It's impossible to tell. He lost a lot of blood.' She glanced out of the window. The two vehicles had been separated and the ambulances stood by, their engines running. 'They will have tried to stabilise him before moving off,' she sighed, turning back to look at the young woman sitting beside her. 'It was a head-on collision, wasn't it?'

'We think so, by the skid marks. They were travelling at speed and on a blind corner. Here's your colleague now.'

Cas was walking towards the car. He was wearing a check shirt hanging loosely around his hips. With weary resignation he leaned his elbow on the roof and looked in. 'He's made it—so far,' he told them. 'But the odds aren't good. He was thrown forward and there was direct impact on the steering-wheel. The dashboard caused injury to his hips, femora and knees.' His voice was thick as he added, 'God knows what his spine is like.'

For a while, all three were silent. 'And loss of blood?' Abbie asked.

He shrugged. 'They brought O-negative with them and sent ahead for cross-matching. We were damn lucky to find that arm.' He glanced at the policewoman and, drawing his hands tiredly over his face, said gruffly, 'If you want statements, we'll be at Tilly House.'

She nodded and Abbie climbed out of the car. The ambulances sped past and Abbie swayed, a wave of dizziness going over her.

He gripped her arm and pulled her against him. 'Hold onto me,' he said.

And she did.

All the way home.

*   *   *

'How did you hurt yourself?' Cas asked as they entered the house.

She hadn't been thinking about the faint stinging coming from her calves. She hadn't been thinking about anything, except that man… trapped…and bleeding and utterly helpless. 'It must have been when I was running,' she answered stupidly. 'I can't really remember.'

'I'd better look at you.' He urged her toward the surgery.

'I'm OK—really.'

'You're bleeding. You just can't see the backs of your legs. They'll blow up like balloons if you're not careful.'

She gave in, more out of vanity than caution, and he pointed to the couch as he stood at the basin. 'Up you jump and I'll see what the damage is.'

She sat on it gingerly, reluctant to swing up her legs 'You needn't bother with the little ones—' she began, then jumped. 'Ouch!'

He turned, still drying his hands. 'What is it?'

'Perhaps you're right. It's my left leg…'

He came over, took hold of her ankles and lifted them. Then he pushed her gently back and grinned. 'And you can let go of that now.' He prised away the blanket and threw it over the chair.

'Don't worry,' he told her dryly, 'I'll try to avoid the knife.'

She didn't think that was funny and jumped as he touched her legs.

'No tights to wrestle with,' he remarked as he frowned at her long, softly tanned legs. 'We're off to a good start.' She could see him smirking as he added, 'They say doctors make the worst patients…'

She decided not to argue since she was the one lying down. His fingers skimmed over her calves and ankles and she tried to ignore the ripples of pleasure flowing over her skin. It wasn't easy. It had something to do with the way he touched her, such large hands with such delicate fingers and a way of…

She swallowed, trying to sit up, but he pushed her back again, this time wagging a finger. 'Wriggly little thing aren't you? Now, stay where you are, or I'll make you suffer.'

'Bully,' she mumbled, but stayed still all the same.

He was gentle and patient and didn't seem to mind when she yelped as he plucked skilfully with the tweezers and applied antiseptic. Occasionally a little twirl of pleasure revolved in her stomach as his fingers brushed soothingly against her skin. Justified pleasure, she decided—as compensation for pain.

Abbie kept noticing his hair. The way it curled wildly down his neck. And how dark it was, not deep brown but ebony. And his skin was tanned—quite deeply—with an even naturalness that suggested it rarely changed shades. In all seasons his dark good looks would remain. Those brooding eyes would always gaze out under heavy, mysterious lids…

'I suggest waiting a bit until you shower,' he was saying as she dragged her attention back. 'They'll sting.'

She croaked her thanks and scrambled off the couch. 'Do you think the police will need statements?' she asked, unpleasantly aware that she was still wearing only her slip and skirt.

Cas nodded, his burning gaze doing little to restore her composure. 'If they come here, you'll have to tell them where I am.'

She looked at him blankly.

'Next door,' he reminded her, jerking his head sideways. 'In the cabin.'

'Oh…' She bit her lip. 'I'd forgotten.'

He frowned. 'Had you indeed?'

'I meant…' She lifted her shoulders and shivered. 'Cas, I was angry and upset last week.

Mostly at what you said about Dad not wanting me here.'

He sighed softly as he perched on the desk, crossing one long leg over the other and folding his arms. 'I shouldn't have said it. I'm sorry.'

She looked at him under her lashes. 'You don't have to stay in the cabin.'

'Are you asking me back?' His dark eyes held hers.

She shivered, dignity impossible in a slip and skirt. 'Do you want to come back?'

'It depends,' he answered her quietly. 'Have you changed your mind because you can't manage without my help? Or because you now accept I haven't tried to cheat you out of house and home? Or should that be practice and land?'

'Quite honestly,' she admitted, 'it's more to do with today.'

'The accident?'

She nodded. 'That poor man, if he survives, may not walk again. Or ever look the same or feel the same again. And it's just a short three months we're arguing over. Three months before you and I move on.'

'You've decided to go back to America, then?'

'Yes.' Her answer was as much as a surprise to herself as Cas, she realised. The decision had been unconscious, but it was the right one. Every

patient she had treated during the week were sup-
porters of Cas's new development. What purpose
could Tilly House fill for them when it was built?

'What about here?'

'I'll probably sell the house. There won't be
any reason to keep it.'

'Are you sure that's what you want to do?' he
asked her frowningly.

She paused, her green eyes staring up at him.
'It's what Dad wanted, isn't it?'

She held her breath as he slowly raised his
eyes. 'Your father knew the medical system was
changing, Abbie. It was why he sold me the land.
But, then,' he added stiffly, 'you only have my
word for that.'

'And my patients'.'

'I see,' he muttered thickly. 'And, of course,
you can take *their* word.'

She made no reply. A part of her still hurt, still
resented this man and what he had achieved in
her absence. Tilly House had always been her
home, the practice was the cornerstone of her
life. But now she had to move on.

There was no other way.

Suddenly Cas stood up. He walked towards
her, swinging out an arm on the way to retrieve
the blanket, then fold it gently round her shoulders. 'You're shivering again,' he murmured.

She wasn't shivering from the cold. She knew exactly why her body was reacting this way. It was because she had lowered her defences and Cas had walked right over them.

Again.

CHAPTER FOUR

IN THE days that followed the accident, it came as a relief, Abbie had to admit, to have Cas back in the house.

She knew almost every patient but she was out of touch. General practice had changed. The demands that were made in a small community were tough. And getting tougher.

So they made an arrangement with Greg Wise's practice in the next village to take calls and some night duties. She wondered how Cas had managed on his own. And, apparently, looking after Dad, too.

Working with him at the accident had given her a new perspective. She listened more attentively to what her patients said.

And she was resigned.

Tilly House was redundant, ill-equipped and unworkable. A one-man surgery just wasn't feasible any more. It probably hadn't been for a long time. It was just that she had never thought about it changing.

Ignorance was bliss, she decided, at least in theory.

It was at the end of May on a warm, overcast Saturday when Abbie was called to Tilly House Tearooms.

The scene she discovered when she arrived was chaotic. The tranquil little restaurant was buzzing with chatter. A pickpocket had circulated the market and people were still examining the contents of their bags.

'Sorry to have to call you out,' Gilli Gaile, proprietor of the tearooms, said as Abbie walked in. Gilli explained the morning's drama as they walked towards the rear room. 'Eve Tredlow fainted. She's all right now, but I didn't like to let her leave. She's a bit unsteady on her feet. She has her granddaughter with her, but…er…' Gilli hesitated. 'The girl is rather…quiet.'

Abbie followed Gilli into a small storeroom adjacent to the kitchen. It was furnished with just a chair and table and mountains of junk. An elderly lady sat at the table and a young girl stood beside her.

'Ignore the mess,' Gilli told Abbie. 'I'll find you a chair from the restaurant.'

'No, that's not necessary, Gilli. You carry on. I'll see to Mrs Tredlow.'

'If you're sure…?'

Abbie nodded and Gilli smiled her thanks.

'Abbie, is that you?' Mrs Tredlow, a smart, grey-haired woman dressed in an expensively tailored suit, peered at Abbie curiously. 'My dear, I haven't seen you for years.'

Abbie smiled warmly as she placed her case on the table and grasped the elderly lady's hand.

'I'm sorry to hear of your sad loss...' Eve Tredlow said.

'Thank you.' Abbie glanced at the teenager and smiled. 'You must be Charlotte.'

'You remember her?' Mrs Tredlow said in surprise before the girl could reply.

'No, we've never met. But Gilli said your granddaughter was with you. And I knew Jane has only one daughter.'

'How lovely to be blessed with such a good memory,' Eve sighed, then glanced at the teenager. 'Charlie's staying with me for the summer. She's just finished college and doesn't quite know what she's going to do with her life.'

Beneath a frond of plaited dark hair, generously sprinkled with coloured beads, a pair of large violet eyes gazed up at Abbie.

'Hi,' Charlie murmured shyly, and Abbie smiled again. She noticed that the baggy jumper and denim jacket hid a tiny frame. She weighed less than eight stone herself, but this girl was certainly nowhere near that. And, as Charlie crossed the room, Abbie noticed something else…

'I'll be outside, Nanna,' the girl said and, without glancing at Abbie, opened the door and vanished.

'Poor Charlie,' Eve said hopelessly. 'She misses her mother, you know.'

'Didn't your son-in-law remarry?' Abbie asked uncertainly. She knew that Jane, Eve's daughter, had been killed in a road accident.

'Yes, but the relationship between Charlie and her stepmother isn't good. Stuart—my son-in-law—thought a spell at college might sort the problem out. But Charlie has decided that academic life is not for her. In fact, at eighteen she appears to have little direction.' Eve looked at Abbie. 'However…I mustn't detain you, my dear. I tried to persuade Gilli not to call you.'

Abbie unlatched her case. 'Tell me about your fainting spell.'

'Oh, I'm as fit as flea.' Eve shrugged. 'It was just…well…all the fuss about purses and wallets being stolen that upset me a little.'

Abbie examined Eve, recalling the memories she had of the Tredlows' beautiful house and garden. As a child, she had gone with her father to visit them. Frederick Tredlow had been alive then, a kind man whose lifelong obsession had been his garden.

Abbie vaguely recalled the pretty girl who was their daughter. And the Tredlows' devastation when she'd been killed when Charlie had been a child.

'Your blood pressure is slightly high,' Abbie noted, and glanced at the records. 'I see you're on medication for your thyroid. Have you had a blood test lately?'

'No,' Eve said, and didn't look Abbie in the eye. 'I must get round to it.'

'I'll write you a form,' Abbie said, and perched her thigh on the table to scribble it.

'I've been naughty,' Eve admitted. 'I should have gone six months ago. It was your father's friend—that nice young doctor—who saw me.'

'Dr Darke, you mean?'

'Yes, your father was having some time off and Dr Darke was taking the surgeries.' Eve's voice softened as she gazed into the distance. 'He made your father rest, despite Richard's resistance.'

'I didn't realise Dad was ill,' Abbie said quietly, and Eve flicked her a glance.

'No one did, my dear. Dr Darke was the one who saw there were problems and sent him for tests—' Eve broke off as she frowned and reached out to lay her hand on Abbie's wrist. 'Oh, I do hope you're not blaming yourself, Abbie. Your father was a very independent man. He wouldn't have wanted to worry you.'

'But I was his only daughter,' Abbie protested. 'Miles away in LA.'

'As Richard intended,' Eve said firmly. 'He was so proud of you, working in that wonderful private hospital with all those glamorous patients.'

Abbie bit her lip. 'I wasn't, actually.' She met Eve's curious gaze. 'I left and took a job at a rehabilitation clinic—drug abuse, the other end of the scale to cosmetic surgery. We're funded by a charity and scratch around for staff most of the time. But the work is fantastically rewarding.'

'And your father never knew?'

'I always *meant* to tell him. I didn't want to explain over the phone or by letter. I wanted to come home. But you know Dad, he kept putting me off. It's no excuse—I should have ignored him and jumped on a plane.'

Eve patted her hand. 'These things happen, my dear.' She sat back in the chair and sighed. 'As a matter of fact, when I saw Dr Darke, I enquired after you. He told me that he hoped your father would be making plans for your return.'

'He did?'

Eve nodded. 'But obviously it wasn't to be.'

Abbie was shocked. Had Cas really tried to persuade Dad to send for her? And, if he had, why hadn't Dad done so?

Eve stood up slowly and slid her hand through Abbie's arm. 'I wonder, my dear, are you going my way? If so, I should be most grateful for a lift.'

Abbie stowed both Charlie and Eve into her father's car and made the short drive to Eve's rambling old house. She took care to see Eve safely in and settled on the sofa, but when she returned to the car, Charlie was waiting for her.

'Is Nanna going to be all right?' the girl asked anxiously.

'Your grandmother should have a blood test,' Abbie explained, struck by the girl's concern now they were alone. 'And she's frail, of course, but having you with her helps.'

'I'll make sure she's OK,' Charlie said. 'But she doesn't like me to fuss.'

'Ah.' Abbie smiled. 'My father was the same.'

'He died, didn't he?' Charlie said quietly. 'Nanna told me all about him. And how they'd been friends for years.'

Abbie nodded, aware the girl was slowly coming out of her shell. As an afterthought she gave Charlie her mobile number. 'If you need me, or can't get hold of me at Tilly House, use this number.'

Looking brighter, Charlie tucked the card in a pocket. Satisfied she could do no more, Abbie left the Tredlows' house.

It was past two by the time she returned home. Cas was in the kitchen, dressed in baggy shorts and a white polo shirt. He was tossing a bowl of salad and grinned as she entered. 'Just in time for lunch.'

'How did you know I was coming back?'

'Telepathy.'

A frisson of awareness went over her as his eyes met hers. 'So you can read my mind now?'

'Maybe.' He tossed some spring onions into the salad and she leaned her hip against the cupboard and watched him.

'You might not like what you find there.' She arched an eyebrow.

'I'll take my chances. Though a few weeks ago, I'd have hesitated.'

They were silent for a moment and she watched, her eyes magnetised by the long, tanned fingers playing seductively with the food. His legs moved lightly over the floor and his thonged feet scuffed gently on the stone.

'I'm not certain about telepathy,' she mumbled, feeling defensive, and he laughed.

'Who is?' Like an acrobat, he balanced one plate expertly on top of another. 'The proof's in the pudding. If you'll excuse the pun.'

Abbie smiled. 'Dad used to say that. He never took people at face value. That's what a one-man practice was about. Knowing every patient like family.'

He put down the tray he was holding and moved towards her. 'Your father was a fine man, Abbie. I don't intend to replace him. I couldn't, and wouldn't try.'

'I just can't see how…a polyclinic,' she said, 'could ever have been Dad's vision. I'm sorry. I'm not saying I don't believe you. It's just that I can't get my head around Dad being…this other person. A person I don't apparently know.'

'He was ill, Abbie,' Cas reminded her. 'Your father may have guessed time was in short supply. People do, somehow. A sixth sense, something driving them on to make decisions they wouldn't normally make. Perhaps trying to explain it to you, all at once, was too much. And he just…procrastinated.'

Like me, Abbie thought, suddenly feeling a tad less guilty. Perhaps Dad's motives had run parallel with hers? He'd got in too deep, like she had. Glib explanations weren't fair. She had needed time, and the right place to explain. Perhaps he had, too.

She stared searchingly into his face. 'Do you really think so?'

'Mmm. I do.'

His gaze lingered on her face, then flickered over her pale green summer dress, bought from one of LA's trendy little boutiques on her first week in the States. A dress which had seemed impossibly expensive. But it had, fleetingly, compensated for homesickness. Besides, she'd had enough funds then.

It was only when she'd started at the clinic that she'd had to scrimp and save. How ironic, when Cas was probably thinking how spoilt she was. How she'd been spoon fed and cosseted. How she'd selfishly neglected her father.

How was he to know that she'd hated the high-profile job her father had been so proud of? Or that she'd thrown it up and moved from her over-sized waterfront apartment and bunked with two other girls downtown. How they'd driven her to distraction with their weird friends and wacky music, yet she'd not regretted one single moment...

'Abbie?'

Cas was staring at her. 'Sorry...?'

He rolled his eyes. 'We need feeding. Come on. Let's eat in the garden.'

She was relieved to watch him sweep up the tray and walk out to the garden. She followed with the bread and drinks and wondered if now would be a good time to talk. Really talk. About LA. About the surgery. About his damned poly-clinic.

But as they reached the wooden table in the garden, she heard herself saying, 'I've been to the village. To Gilli Gaile's.'

Procrastinating again…

'That little restaurant in the market square?' he asked, lowering the tray and setting two places.

'Yes. One of Dad's elderly patients, Eve Tredlow, fainted in the restaurant.'

'Eve?' He cast her a frown. 'It was Eve who lost her daughter, wasn't it? She died just before I came to Tilly.'

Abbie nodded, placing the bread and drinks on the mats. 'I didn't know Jane or her family very well. They moved away. But my parents were close friends of the Tredlows—Dad especially, after Mum died.' A soft breeze blew and Abbie caught the dizzy drift of aftershave. 'Jane,' she made herself continue, 'left a husband and young daughter. And it's Charlie who's staying with Eve at the moment.'

'That's great for Eve, isn't it?'

Abbie followed him back into the kitchen where he rescued baked potatoes from the oven. When they got back to the garden, she sat at the table and he plopped one onto her plate.

'Looks good.'

'Healthy eating. Potatoes in their jackets. Your father loved them.'

She nodded, glancing at him as he sat down. 'He did, didn't he?' She smiled softly. 'At least we agree there.'

He gave her salad and didn't comment—not until they began eating, when he said, 'What were you saying about Eve and Charlie?'

Abbie sighed. 'I noticed something about Charlie and I can't think what it was. She's a quiet girl, rather thin. Adores her grandmother, too.'

He grunted. 'Aren't all teenagers thin and quiet? Either that or totally mad.'

She hid a smile. 'Yes, but there was something more. I just don't know what it was.'

'How long have you known Eve?' he asked, piling on more salad.

'All my life. I used to go with Dad on visits to their house. They had a fabulous garden. Mr

Tredlow let me pick from the fruit trees. And there was a swing…hanging from one of the trees. I suppose it was Jane's. I was only about ten, so it really appealed.'

She looked up and saw he was watching her. His eyes were a deep and luxurious brown, though now in the sunshine she could see the tiny black flecks that made them so dark and brooding.

His gaze rested on her face and her hand went up automatically to hide the shower of freckles sprinkled on her nose. He saw the gesture and wagged a fork in her face.

'Don't squint, use these.' He dropped the fork and fished in his pocket. He brought out some sunglasses and slid them on her nose. Lifting her hair behind her ear, he tucked the ends of the shades into place. 'Better?'

'Mmm.' His thumb glanced against her ear. A shiver rippled all the way down her spine.

'Come on, eat up.' He smiled. 'We'll talk about Eve and Charlie afterwards. Oh, and before I forget, I phoned the hospital today about the two casualties from the accident. The girl was discharged the following day. And the guy, a thirty-two-year-old salesman, is going to make it. He'll need months of physio, but they saved his legs and spine and patched up the rest.'

Abbie nodded slowly. 'I wonder if he—or she—knows how lucky they are.'

Cas got stuck into his meal, muttering something about no one ever appreciating luck until they didn't have it.

'What was it that disturbed you so much about Charlie?' he asked eventually, scooping a last crumb from his plate.

'How do you know I was disturbed?' Abbie tilted her head. 'I mean, rather than just…well, concerned.'

'Body language.'

'Body language.' She took a slice of apple that he had cut for her and slid it slowly between her lips.

He gave her a crooked smile. 'It's these…' Casually, he reached across the table and took her hands. 'You're usually quite economical with movement. Until you get flustered. Then, your hands kind of…give off messages…'

She couldn't withdraw her fingers. They'd frozen or melted into his—she wasn't sure which.

'And…that's what happened when I came back from Eve's?' she mumbled.

'Uh-huh.'

'So now you can read my thoughts *and* body language?' She glanced doubtfully under her lashes.

'More or less.'

'So what am I thinking now?' she challenged—foolishly.

'Do you really want me to tell you?'

She held her breath as he leaned forward, circling her palm with his thumb. One dark eyebrow was raised, his full lips open and his brow pleated. He continued to stare at her, the dark eyes seeming to burrow their way inside her as she felt his thumb travel outward and over her fingers.

'No,' she croaked and tried to draw her hand away.

'You're thinking,' he continued, tightening his grip, 'that there might be a very small chance I really can read your thoughts.'

She laughed shakily. '*Guess* at them… perhaps.'

'A little more than that, I think.' His eyes sparkled. 'You're wondering what I'm doing here. In your life. And as much as you try to distance yourself,' he went on slowly, licking the curve of his lip in pure satisfaction at her discomfort, 'half of you says it's OK. He's not out to steal the family treasure.'

His words rained gently down on a tender breath that spun over her cheek like silk. The stretch of his long fingers over her hands made her shiver again and for a moment she could al-most—*almost*—believe he was reading her mind.

'There isn't a lot left to steal.' She said it mostly to fight the sensations that were making her head swim. And knew at once she'd shot herself in the foot.

'I'm wasting my time—obviously,' he snorted. He dropped her hands and muttered something under his breath.

'Cas, I only meant—'

'I know what you meant.' He stood up, piled the plates noisily on top of one another and strode into the house.

Annoyed with herself, she gathered the rest of the stuff and followed him in. Why couldn't she have just kept her mouth closed? And sat there. And enjoyed it.

No, she had to harp back to their old problems. Well, her old problem.

'I'll do the washing up,' she said contritely as she walked into the kitchen.

'You can't until I fix the boiler.' He was on all fours and his head had disappeared into a cup-board beneath the sink. When he emerged, he was holding her father's toolbox.

'Is it the boiler?' she asked vaguely.

'No, the whole damned system.'

'What's wrong with it?'

'Everything.'

'It's always been a bit iffy…'

'Iffyness has nothing to do with it. It's antique and you can't get any parts because it's obsolete.'

'So what will we do?' she asked lamely.

'Pray,' he muttered as he slouched out. 'And don't run any water or we'll get an air lock.'

She dodged the tentacles of anger as he passed. A little pang of remembrance tightened her throat as she glanced at the toolbox.

Then regret followed.

Regret. That she'd said there wasn't much left to steal. Which had been unkind. But now she had to live with it, because bringing it up again would only make him angrier. And they'd fight.

So she went upstairs to her room, ignoring the cursing from the attic. She pulled on her jogging pants and left the house. But the jog turned into a sprint as she ran down the lane to the sea and tried to forget what she'd said.

Sunday was avoidance day.

And it worked. Abbie lurked in the house and he went next door. From the bedroom window she saw a bright yellow hard hat bobbing up and down in the field. One little dot of realism…

On Monday morning an emergency took Caspar out. Abbie took a blissfully peaceful surgery and patients flowed in happily until lunch-time. Afterwards, she drove into Tilly and bought groceries. She'd made a note of what was in the cupboard—tinned tuna and salmon, pasta and umpteen assorted tins of beans. So she bought lots of fresh and frozen food to accompany what they already had in.

'Like some?' she offered when Cas strolled in at suppertime. 'Or are you eating at the pub?'

'What is it?' he asked irritably.

'Grilled sole and salad. And new potatoes.' She lifted out the fish and flashed the soft brown coating of butter, gently sizzling.

He looked mildly impressed. 'OK.' He shrugged and sat down to watch her.

It was a start, she told herself hopefully.

'What was the emergency this morning?'

'Reggie Donaldson, the auctioneer. Laryngitis and a panic attack, poor man.'

'Which came first?'

'He's had a blazing throat for weeks, and he's worrying about work.'

'He used to run the cattle market,' Abbie re-called. 'It was a blow when it all finished.'

'Well, either he takes it easy or he's going to be doing nothing at all,' Cas remarked shortly. 'At least, not with his voice. I'm getting the throat checked out.'

Abbie turned. 'Tests?'

Cas nodded, stretching out his long tanned legs under green Bermudas. 'The infection is too recurrent.'

Abbie swirled the potatoes absently. 'I saw Diana Moore this morning. She's had her hysterectomy. Says to say she's starting to feel much better. And Lennie Marins—the young man with gingivitis?'

'And some.' Cas whistled through his teeth. 'How is he?'

'Smiling,' Abbie grinned. 'He went to the dentist for the first time in a decade. The hygienist had a field day with all that plaque.'

Cas laughed aloud. 'I told him he'd be a lonely old man if he didn't. He's got his eye on the barmaid at The Crow, so he must have taken my advice.'

'You mean he didn't come to surgery?'

'We had a bar consultation,' Cas replied, idly leaning forward. He rested his chin on his hand to watch her. 'And it seems to have worked.'

'Do you eat every night at the pub?' She tried not to catch his gaze, which seemed to be hovering below the tie of the apron. She'd wound her hair into a knot at the nape of her neck and tied the apron over her shorts. But she felt his

eyes and dropped the spatula on the hob. It crackled furiously.

'Not always. It depends.'

'On what?' She retrieved the spatula and
frowned at him.

'On whether you're using the kitchen.'

The penny dropped and she sighed. 'Aren't
you overreacting a bit?'

His dark eyes shimmered. 'Going on our track
record, no.'

'You're welcome to share,' she said, and wondered if it had been her who had spoken so
rashly. 'There's always enough for two.'

One dark eyebrow twitched. 'Bribing the enemy? Isn't that dangerous?'

She supposed she had sarcasm coming, so she
ignored him and spooned the fish and potatoes
onto plates. Then placed it on the table in front
of him.

They ate in silence, but Cas was ravenous and
rapidly cleared his plate. Afterwards she scooped
out ice cream in fluffy pink and white blobs.
When that had disappeared and they had managed not to inflict any more verbal damage on
one another, she made coffee.

'Delicious,' he managed. 'Thanks.'

'That's OK.'

'Do we fight over the washing-up?'

Abbie shook her head. 'No, you can do it. I've cooked.'

He pulled a face and she wished she'd offered to wipe up. It would be nice, in an old-fashioned way, to stand at the sink and talk. But she found herself at the door and was opening it.

'Cas?' She turned to see him tying on the apron, and her heart gave a tug.

'What?'

She gulped. 'Nothing.'

He glowered and she walked out. Then she poked her head round the door again and the words tumbled out. But if they hadn't she would have made a pig's ear of it.

'About the other night. About nothing left to steal. I'm sorry. That was unfair. And I didn't mean it.'

She dodged out, not waiting for a reaction. Maybe he hadn't even heard. But she felt better. And that night when she lay in bed and heard him climb the stairs, her heart stopped still.

Did he pause on the landing?

Or was it her imagination?

Or was it the plumbing? The same old plumbing that had gurgled away in the house for years, but which was now hanging in by a wing and a prayer and the ministrations of the man in the room above.

CHAPTER FIVE

HOWARD BAILEY arrived at surgery on a glorious morning. Without a puff, he walked in, sat down and beamed at Abbie.

'How's this then, for size?' He gestured to his stomach. 'I'm down to thirteen stone and feeling great.'

'How?' Abbie asked, though she suspected it had something to do with Cas.

'Well, I saw Dr Darke a day or two after you called,' Howard explained. 'I was in a right flummox, worrying about my weight. And I told him so. All because I couldn't resist going into George Lambert's for his wonderful bread every day.'

Abbie nodded, though when she glanced at the records, she could see no mention of the consultation.

'I took up fishing again,' Howard went on cheerfully. 'I abandoned it years ago because of the wife, who couldn't abide fish. I told Dr Darke a story once about how I caught a lobster which came back to life in the sink and scared her witless. Well, it was zilch fish after that. But Dr

Darke suggested, as I'm on my own now, I should give it another crack. Eat as much fish as I could catch. Sort of hone the taste buds. Fish is fantastic for the heart. Look at all those professional footballers—they're often on fish diets. Fit lot they are. And no wonder.'

'Don't you eat any bread at all now?' Abbie asked, wondering where the idea of footballers diets had sprung from. And thinking she had more than an inkling of the answer.

'Wholemeal.' Howard grinned. 'George brings a small loaf twice a week. Don't go in to the shop. Too much temptation.'

'And your outpatients appointment?' Abbie asked, half expecting Howard to make an excuse.

'I'd lost eight pounds when I went. Got a gold star.' He chuckled. 'I reckon the doc won't recognise me in three months. Anyway, thank you, lass, for what you did. You started the ball rolling with that fresh appointment.'

'It appears to be Dr Darke…' Abbie shrugged '…who's sorted you out, not me.'

'It was the pair of you,' her patient insisted. 'You make a good team. Now, all I want is my pills and I'll get out from under your feet.'

Abbie made out Howard's regular prescription and saw him to the front door. 'Has Dr Darke seen you—recently?' she asked cautiously.

'No. I thought I might bump into him today.' Howard raised an eyebrow. 'Out with the girl-friend, is he? The one with the swanky little mo-tor?'

Abbie felt an odd little gripe at her ribs and ignored it. 'Not as far as I know,' she said, and glanced at her watch. 'Wait if you like. He shouldn't be long.'

Howard gave her a long, narrowed stare then shrugged. 'I won't stop, thanks all the same. I'm going out on the boat this afternoon with a cou-ple of pals. Can't let the big one get away.' He laughed as he walked away. 'I'll leave you to pass on the good news.'

Thanks, Howard, Abbie thought grudgingly. And followed her patient's departure with thoughtful eyes. So Cas had gone to see Howard after all...

And not mentioned it!

She went back to the desk and glanced at Howard's records to make certain she hadn't missed anything.

Not a word.

'*Trust* me, the man says,' Abbie muttered dis-dainfully. 'And then he does something like this!'

Unhelpfully, a mental picture formed of Cas reclining in a sleek little sports car, his dark hair falling over his forehead, a smile of satisfaction spreading over his lips. A leggy blonde was driving him, her head tossed back and her hair streaming in the wind. Or was she an exotic brunette—or fiery redhead?

Abbie realised she'd been too busy swallowing her outrage to quiz Howard more on a subject that apparently held more than a passing interest for him. Whoever she was, the girlfriend had obviously engaged Howard's thoughts to a considerable degree.

And, damn it, was now engaging hers!

She saw two more patients, sorted out the appointments for the following day and cleared the desk. Then she sat in the garden and thought about Howard. Again. Why hadn't Cas told her he'd visited him? And, most important of all, why hadn't he written the visit on the records?

Guilty conscience. Must be.

She was surprised he hadn't cancelled the hospital appointment she'd made for Howard! She couldn't believe he'd gone behind her back and called on Howard and then not written it on the records.

She had worked herself into quite a stew by the time Cas arrived back. Which was late. She was in the office, trying to make sense of the latest NHS guidelines on some obscure aspects of health, when he walked in, all smiles.

'You're late,' she said, and wished she hadn't. Which he was swift to pick up on, of course.

'For what?' The smile on his full lips slightly wilted into wariness. But he kept it plastered there. And ran a hand through his somewhat untidy pelt of hair, his fingers lingering pensively on his neck as he met her gaze.

'Just late. It's five and usually you're back by then.'

The smile reinforced itself as he perched a thigh on the corner of the desk. He was wearing jeans. New ones by the looks of it, that hugged his long legs with a spectacular familiarity.

The shirt could have been new, too, she decided as she glanced at the crisp white creases. Turned-back cuffs that looked almost indecently sexy. Forearms to slay a bear with and little swirls of black hair clinging gamely to the muscle. And those big, broad hands, brown as berries with a smattering of hair nudging down to the knuckles. A gold watch, glistening on tanned skin…

Abbie shot herself a bolt of loathing. How could she be thinking like this when she was so disgusted at his behaviour? She looked down for Howard's notes, which she was about to fling at him. Subtly, of course. Then panicked. What had she done with them?

'Yes, well, I had a puncture,' she heard him saying—in a satisfactorily defensive tone. 'I had to change it with the spare. It took me longer than I thought.' He stretched and changed position on the desk. Then she felt rather than saw him sink into the chair. Four or maybe five safe feet away. 'Busy morning?' he added smilingly.

'Not really.' She burrowed under the correspondence frantically.

'What are you looking for?'

'Nothing.' Where were those damn records?

'You're getting a bit wound up for nothing.'

She threw him a withering glance. 'I'm not. Not at all.'

'Yes, you are,' he countered. 'Your hands are at it again. Look at them.'

'My hands are moving because they *have* to. Why have we always got so much rubbish in here? Why don't we throw it out?'

'I do. But you're a hoarder.'

'I am not.' She twisted in the swivel chair and peered under the desk. All she could see was a pair of very long legs covered in denim, one ankle crossed over the other. 'I trash all the rubbish—usually,' she moaned, attempting to drag back her concentration and bumping her head instead.

'Are these what you're looking for?'

A set of dog-eared patient records waggled in her face.

'Where did you find them?'

'Under there.' He jerked his head toward the pile of NHS correspondence.

'Thank you,' she said formally, not missing the satisfied expression on his face. Well, it wouldn't stay there for very long. At least not when she told him who they belonged to.

'So Howard's been in,' he mused, stealing her thunder.

Her jaw dropped. 'Yes,' she admitted reluctantly.

'And…?'

'And…and,' she began, flustered by his reaction, 'and he told me you visited him and gave him a diet and said something about footballers and how fit they are, and when I look in here…' she jabbed a self-righteous finger at the records '…there wasn't a word. Not one single word about you going to see him and—'

'Have you finished?' he interrupted her quietly.

'No, I haven't,' she answered crossly. 'I mean, OK, we had a fight about me getting Howard that new appointment before he lost weight. But even so, how could you go behind my back?'

'I didn't.'

'You did,' she gasped. 'Howard said you visited after I'd seen him.'

'No, he didn't,' he argued stubbornly. 'You've got it muddled. Either that or Howard's telling a lie and I don't believe he would.'

She stared at him, her green eyes doing things which she knew they were doing but which she couldn't stop. Spitting green fire just didn't gel with calm. And she wanted to do calm—and control—and poise, at this moment. Which she wasn't. Because, as usual, Cas was successfully winding her up.

She braced her shoulders. 'Look at his records. You didn't write a word down about your visit. You couldn't, could you? Because you sneaked in after I'd seen Howard and—'

To her humiliation, he began to laugh. A rich, deep, echoing sound that came up from his stomach and into his throat with a slow, unstoppable growl of mirth. That would have, under other circumstances, sounded disturbingly sexy.

'What's so funny?' she demanded, going scarlet.

'You really think I could do that?' he asked incredulously. 'Go behind your back, as you call it?'

It was a second or two before Abbie replied as she watched his body fold itself into unhelpfully relaxed lines, his long legs somehow curling themselves into an incredibly masculine pose, one heel heaved up and resting on a lethargic thigh, his fingers playing languorously on the side of his knee. Completely unfazed.

'Well, didn't you?' she challenged, tossing back her cloud of auburn curls.

'No,' he said quietly. 'I didn't *visit* Howard.'

'You did. You—'

'Think, Abbie.' He cut her short. 'Did Howard say I'd visited him? Or did he say that he simply saw me?'

She hadn't expected that question. Was there any difference? And could she remember anyway?

She couldn't.

As though reading her mind, which she was still terrified he could do, he said, 'It's true I saw Howard.'

'Ah!' She preened.

'But I didn't visit him. Our meeting was quite by chance. In the pub.'

Abbie struggled with her pride and failed as she replied curtly, 'You seem to treat more people in the pub than you do in surgery.'

'That's not fair,' he said. And she knew it wasn't.

'Sorry,' she mumbled, though not sincerely.

'Accepted.'

'So it was in the pub you decided on the fishing thing, did you?' She couldn't keep the irony from her voice. 'Over a pint and a bit of bonding.'

'Not a pint,' he told her carefully. 'Howard isn't into beer, just pastries and bread. I suggested he have the prawns instead of the pie he'd ordered, and one thing led to another. I threw in something ridiculous about professional footballers and obviously Howard took note. And that was it. Nothing underhand at all. Promise.'

She lifted her eyes to his. 'I suppose I did get it a bit muddled.'

'Yes,' he agreed, 'just a bit.'

She wished there was a convenient hole to drop into. Luckily the phone on the desk rang and she answered it.

'Susan's having pains, but not the usual ones,' Josie Dunning said in a shaky voice. 'I think it's contractions. There's no time to call anyone else. We need you and Dr Darke. And...to be honest…I don't feel very well either, Abbie. I've come over all dizzy.'

'I'll come over straight away,' Abbie said and replaced the phone.

'Susan?' Cas arched a curious eyebrow as Abbie stood up.

'And Josie. She said she feels dizzy.' Abbie frowned. 'And Josie wouldn't say anything unless she really was feeling ill.'

'I'll come with you,' he said, and reached for the phone. 'If Susan's in labour you'll have your hands full.'

'What about cover here?'

'I'm ringing Greg Wise. He'll take any calls until we're back. Oh, and we'll need a couple of maternity packs.'

'OK. I'll see to that.'

Abbie collected all she needed and caught the tail end of Cas's phone conversation as he sorted out cover with the doctor in the next village.

'All done,' he told her, and a few minutes later, electing to take his vehicle, they were on their way to the Dunnings'.

'You didn't finish telling me about Howard,' he said as they rattled their way down the country lane. 'And how much better he looks.'

'How do you know he looks better?' Abbie said in surprise.

'He wouldn't have turned up at the surgery if he hadn't,' Cas replied easily. 'That meal at The Crow? It was on me. The deal was that if he didn't lose weight, he'd have to return the favour—and buy the drinks.'

'You said Howard didn't like beer.'

Cas nodded. 'But mine is champers.'

She smiled until she realised he wasn't joking. 'Is it?'

He nodded. 'When I'm in the mood.' He looked at her quickly and she felt her skin prickle. She didn't ask *what* mood. She already knew.

Nothing stirred in the long sandy drive up to the farmhouse. Years ago, Abbie thought, there would have been cows waiting to be milked in the dairy, and Bess and Gerry, the two farm dogs, would have barked a rapturous welcome. Now Bob Dunning was leasing his land to other farmers and barely scraping a living.

'There's Josie,' Cas said as they scrambled out. Abbie felt sorry for the Dunnings, who were the last of their farming line. Susan's four sisters were scattered far and wide and it was clear that Susan had no love of country life. A farming tradition that had endured for generations had now come to an end. The end of an era, Abbie thought wistfully.

'She's in the bedroom upstairs,' Josie said as they entered. 'There's towels and clean bedsheets. And there's hot water on the sideboard.'

'What about you?' Cas asked quietly, frowning down at Josie's pale face.

'I feel pretty shabby,' Josie admitted, leaning against the door. 'And I can't seem to get my words out properly. They all feel muddled.' She swayed and Cas took her arm and led her slowly back into the sitting room.

'It's OK,' he told Abbie over his shoulder. 'You go on. I'll catch up later.'

Abbie found Susan in her bedroom, propped up by pillows on the old-fashioned bedstead. Abbie washed her hands in the bowl, then set out the maternity pack and examined Susan. She was surprised to see that the baby was well on its way.

'Where's Mum?' Susan gasped, dragging at her damp hair as another contraction came. 'I want her here. The pains are getting worse.'

'Dr Darke's with her.' Abbie eased Susan's tense shoulders back on the pillow. 'Try to relax, Sue. Now, I want you to stop pushing. And pant.'

'I can't,' Susan protested. 'I'm exhausted.'

'Wait for the next contraction and you're almost there,' Abbie assured her. And though Susan complained bitterly throughout, Abbie was able to rotate the baby's head in line with the rest of its body. With the final contraction, one little shoulder slipped through, then the other.

'Is it over?' Susan asked, and Abbie laughed.

'It's over, Sue. You have a gorgeous baby girl.' Abbie cleared the baby's mouth, eyes and ears. They were rewarded by a lusty cry as her tiny fingers curled into her palms.

'She's beautiful.' Susan stared down at her baby and tears began to flow down her cheeks. 'I can't believe I produced something so amazing.'

Abbie nodded. 'Much better than TV.'

Susan laughed. 'I don't think I'll be watching much telly with her around. Mum was right. She said—' Susan stopped and glanced up. 'I'm really worried about Mum. She wanted to see the baby being born.'

Abbie clipped and cut the cord and the placenta came away, occupying Abbie's attention. But as she made Susan comfortable, she wondered what was happening downstairs. Susan was right. Had Josie been well, nothing would have prevented her from witnessing the birth.

'Have you thought of a name yet?' Abbie asked, as Susan held her baby.

'Yes, Joanne, Mum's middle name.'

'Lovely. Well, if you can bear to part with her, I'll check her and make certain everything's OK.'

Susan looked on as Abbie laid Joanne on the bed. 'What are you looking for?' she asked anxiously.

'Really, just clicky hips and the odd heart noise that might not be right,' Abbie explained. 'But she's fine. All we need to do now is weigh her.'

'Mum put some scales there, beside the bed.' Susan pointed to an elderly pair of scales which Josie had prepared with tissue paper. 'We never thought they'd be used as I was down to go into hospital for the delivery.'

'Joanne certainly didn't waste time in arriving.' Abbie smiled as she weighed the baby. 'Just four kilos.' She handed the baby back. 'A good weight, although she'll lose a bit as she adjusts to feeding. She really is a lovely little girl, Sue. Look at that crop of hair.'

'But why is she crying so loudly?' Susan wailed as she rocked the infant in her arms.

'Because she's hungry. Time for her first feed. Do you want me to help you with a clean nightdress?'

'Yes, please.' When that was done, Susan pressed the baby's head against her breast but it wasn't long before she gave up. 'I can't do it!' she exclaimed impatiently. 'She doesn't like my milk. I'm hopeless at it. I never get anything right.'

'Yes, you will. Look.' Abbie grasped the baby's velvety dark head and brushed her tiny mouth against Sue's breast. The baby responded at once, nuzzling in for her milk. 'You see, and when she turns...' Abbie pushed gently. 'Just keep your hand there, supporting her head. Once she gets the idea, you won't have to do anything.'

Susan gasped. 'Oh, Abbie, look at her.'

Abbie sat on the bed and nodded. 'Breastfeeding's wonderful, isn't it?'

'You've got a real knack with babies,' Sue said quietly. 'I remember at school. We had those weird dolls to bath? You really took to it. Not like me. Our teacher said I drowned the poor thing.' They both laughed and Abbie looked at Joanne.

'Now you've got a real baby.'

'And it's wonderful,' Sue murmured.

Abbie nodded thoughtfully. 'Do you remember a midwife coming to school and telling us how she got into nursing?'

Susan shook her head.

'It was through delivering her own mother's baby. She was about fourteen and the experience, she told us, was a revelation. She'd wanted to be a secretary and claimed she'd always passed out at the sight of blood.'

'I wish I'd taken more notice,' Sue sighed. 'I might have enjoyed being pregnant if I'd known what it was really like.'

'You didn't enjoy your pregnancy?' Abbie asked, and Sue shook her head.

'I suppose because Ralf took off and I was pretty depressed for a while. If it hadn't been for Dr Darke, I might not be here today. Or little Joanne.' She shuddered. 'What an awful thought. Right now, I couldn't feel luckier. I used to think I was trapped here at the farm, but Joanne changes all that.' She looked up at Abbie and grinned. 'Hark at me. I must be delirious.'

At that moment, Cas walked in. 'I see congratulations are in order,' he said, and smiled as he bent down to look at the baby.

Susan nodded, her eyes anxiously going to the hall. 'Where's Mum?'

'Resting on the sofa,' Cas said, and flicked a glance at Abbie. 'Have you a moment?'

'There's nothing wrong, is there?' Susan stiffened and the baby's head fell away from her breast. She began to cry loudly.

'If you get upset, Sue, she'll be aware of it, so try to relax.' Abbie helped her with the baby's positioning again.

'Take your time,' Cas said easily, and walked to the door, indicating that Abbie should follow. 'We'll have a chat afterwards.'

He stood waiting for Abbie at the top of the stairs and she knew before he spoke that it was bad news. 'Josie's had a stroke,' he said quietly. 'I'm going to admit her.'

Bob Dunning strode in from the kitchen, slid off his cap and stared at his wife in amazement. 'What's up, love? What's everyone doing here?'

'Sit down, Bob,' Josie whispered as she lay on the sofa. 'Don't get upset.'

'I won't if someone will tell me what's happening.'

'Your wife has had a stroke,' Cas said as he packed away his stethoscope and closed his bag. 'It was a small one, but I'm admitting her to hospital so that we can find out why.' Cas added quietly, 'And your daughter's delivered a beautiful baby girl.'

The tall, heavily built man in a tweed jacket looked nonplussed. He crossed the room and sat on the big sofa beside his wife. He took her hand

and patted it, searching her face. 'I knew you wasn't well. You've been right off colour lately.'

'Bob...don't make a fuss now,' Josie murmured. 'Go and see our Sue.'

'Not until I know about you.'

Cas moved beside him. 'There's not a lot I can tell you at the moment. We won't know the cause until we've done some tests. That's why I'm sending your wife to hospital. Once we know the reasons why, we can start taking precautions so it doesn't happen again.'

'You mean she has to go *now*?' Bob looked bewildered.

Cas nodded. 'Do you want to go with her?'

'Course I do.' Emotion filled his face and he glanced at Abbie. 'What about Sue and her baby? What's to be done about them?'

'I think Sue would like you to see the baby,' Abbie said quietly. 'And we haven't told her about Josie.'

Bob stood up. 'I'll break the news. And I'll pack a few things for Jo.'

'What will happen to Susan?' Josie whispered after her husband had gone.

'We'll sort something out,' Cas said reassuringly. 'You aren't to worry.'

'How long will they keep me in?' She turned to Abbie.

'It depends. They'll try to find out why you've had this little blip.'

The sound of a siren in the distance caused Cas to go to the front door, and very soon an ambulance was waiting outside. After Josie had been transferred to it, Cas helped Bob with a battered case and a few carrier bags.

'What about Sue?' Bob asked again as the paramedic closed the rear door.

'Don't worry,' Abbie reassured him. 'We'll take care of Sue and the baby.'

'*We*?' Cas murmured as the ambulance disappeared.

'What else could I say?' Abbie shrugged.

Susan's voice rang out upstairs and Cas rolled his eyes. 'I'll go,' he said, and crooked an eyebrow. 'This time.'

Abbie cleaned the bowls in the kitchen and wondered how Bob and Susan were going to cope without Josie. She was still thinking about it when Cas walked in, holding the baby.

Abbie peered over his arm. 'All fed?'

'Up to the brim.' He grinned and stroked a tender finger against the pink cheek. A pair of crinkled lids flickered above a snub nose and tiny fingers curled in contentment.

Perfect, Abbie thought breathlessly as Cas met her eyes. She saw something in his face, though she couldn't have said what. She ached for the moment to last, but again Susan's voice echoed down.

'Your turn.' Cas pressed the baby into her arms. 'I'll sort out the social worker and the midwife. See what they can come up with.'

'How is Josie—really?' Abbie asked as he went.

'Sick,' he admitted gruffly. 'I doubt whether this little episode will be the last. Her BP was off the wall. They'll need to do the full bunch of tests.'

'Bob and Susan are going to have to pull their weight,' Abbie decided firmly.

He nodded. 'My sentiments exactly.'

As Abbie went upstairs, a vision of the Dunnings trying to cope without Josie made her shudder. And when she entered the bedroom, all hope disappeared.

Susan was in tears.

Again.

CHAPTER SIX

'TIRED?'

'Not really.'

'Liar.' Cas stopped the car outside Tilly House and chuckled. 'You're shattered.'

Abbie stretched, her body aching for rest. 'If you must know, I'm not even looking forward to climbing the stairs.'

He laughed softly as he switched off the engine. 'Susan certainly kept you at it.'

Abbie sighed, her body relaxed into the seat. So relaxed, she felt as if she could sleep there. 'I had no idea farmhouse stairs were so steep.'

'Bet you're pleased you didn't volunteer to stay the night.'

Abbie nodded. 'How do you think they'll manage?'

'Perfectly well,' Cas said, and jumped out, coming round to open her door. 'Here…watch your step. It's dark.' She reached out and he grasped her hand.

'I should know where I'm going,' she grumbled as they picked their way to the front door.

His grip was strong and warm and she wished it would stay there…

She tried not to think about his hands and the sprinkling of dark hair that covered them and grazed against her fingertips. She tried and failed as the night breeze trailed over her skin and a hundred different scents filled the air under the full moon.

'Watch out. There's a bit of crazy paving,' he warned as he guided her round. His outline was tall, firm—familiar in the darkness. And something else. Something she didn't want to dwell on because under the tiredness her stomach was revolving wildly. 'Do you think Marjorie Ellis will survive the night?' she asked, trying not to think at all.

'Oh, she's a tough old bird. It was lucky she rang whilst we were there. I'd no idea Josie had a sister living in Tilly.'

'No, neither did I,' Abbie murmured. 'Apparently they haven't spoken in years.'

'Ah, well, she seemed to jump at the chance of helping out. Perhaps she's glad of the company,' Cas suggested as they reached the front door. 'Odd things, families.'

'Hmm. I s'pose.' Abbie yawned as Cas thrust his key in the lock. The porch light went on and she blinked. 'Home,' she sighed. 'Wonderful.'

Cas let go of her hand and disappeared into the office. She stood there, rubbing the spot on her wrist. It felt warm and tingling and if she hadn't been so tired...

'No calls from Greg Wise,' Cas shouted. 'I'll ring him first thing.'

Abbie realised she was hungry, then banished the thought. Now she looked at the stairs, she couldn't wait to climb them. Bed seemed ludicrously attractive. She had a twinge of sympathy for Sue in that big farmhouse, trying to adjust to being a new mother. Marjorie Ellis had never had babies and was a spinster. And Bob, well, he was as helpless as a kitten without Josie. No one would have thought it, but he was. As Cas had said—funny things, families.

Cas reappeared. A dark shadow was creeping over his jaw. He looked wild and ruffled and incredibly sexy, and she wondered what it would be like to walk up those stairs, hand in hand.

'Sleep well,' he said, and she nodded.

'Cas?'

'Hmm?' He was staring down at her with those dark, deliciously brown eyes and she almost forgot what she was going to say.

'Can I ask you something?'

'At this time of night?' He leaned against the banister and just about managed not to roll his eyes.

'Eve said something to me,' she blurted. 'And it's been on my mind.'

'What?' he shrugged.

'She said that you once told her that you hoped Dad would be making plans for my return.'

He narrowed his gaze as his mouth twitched. 'And what if I did?'

'Why did you hope that?'

'It's an odd question, isn't it?' he asked defensively.

'Not really. Can you remember telling Eve that?'

He nodded slowly. 'No doubt I'm incriminating myself by admitting it but, yes, I can remember.' There was an awkward pause before he added carefully, 'Your father had this idealised idea of your career. He felt you shouldn't be distracted from it at any cost. That his illness came way down the line of priorities. I didn't see it that way and I urged him to call you back from the States.'

'I wish you'd succeeded in convincing him,' she sighed. 'I wanted to come home. I'd been trying for ages and he kept making excuses.' She met his gaze and for a moment neither of them spoke.

When he did, his voice was soft and husky. 'I know that now.'

'Then,' she herself croaking, 'that's all that matters.'

He pushed his hand up slowly into his hair and inhaled. Letting out a long and slow breath, he murmured, 'I'm sorry I misread the situation. And I shouldn't have interfered. I should know enough about life to realise that—'

'Families are funny things,' she said, and smiled softly.

'Yes.' He nodded. 'They certainly are.'

She swallowed. 'Well, goodnight, then. Sleep well.'

'You, too.'

For a few seconds they seemed frozen, the tick of the clock in the hall making little circles in the air around them. Then, as if in slow motion, he leaned forward and kissed her. On the forehead, so softly and meltingly that his lips hardly seemed real.

Then he paused and his breath trailed over her and she trembled. She wanted to respond but would she recover from a kiss if she did? Could she be dreaming? Perhaps she was. But even so she didn't want to let go, so she stayed where she was, her face tilted up, his lips moving down to her mouth.

Then he kissed her again, on the lips, and she felt her hands go up to his shoulders and stay there. Don't wake up, Abbie Scott, she prayed. If it's a dream, let it go on for ever. And ever. Please.

But she knew it wouldn't. And when she opened her eyes, he was staring down at her, his face thrown into hard relief by the porch light.

Gradually he straightened and pulled back. 'Night,' he said gruffly. 'I'll lock up.'

She wanted to do something. Say something. But she couldn't think what. Instead, she nodded. 'OK. Thanks,' she mumbled, and went up the stairs.

Abbie opened the door of her room and walked in, closing it behind her with almost reverent care. She sat on the bed, waiting for whatever was going on under her ribs to subside.

Then she laid her fingers on her mouth. And closed her eyes.

And wished for more. Much, much more.

Everything was fine, Abbie told herself the next morning when she woke. Under control.

She showered, dressed in her working clothes and kept telling herself so. And was still assuring herself as she came downstairs.

Cas was in the kitchen.

A CD was playing, unusually—something unbearably cheerful for seven in the morning. There was the smell of herbs and the scent of grass, or maybe it was hay, drifting in from the open window.

Abbie's mind went alarmingly blank. Was it her turn for surgery or was it his? Tuesday—so it was hers. And Cas would be doing calls, if there were any.

She moved suspiciously towards the open kitchen door. The aroma was stunning. Mixed herbs...olive oil. A pan was sizzling on the hob, an omelette fluffed inside it. 'Hi.' He turned, waving a spatula in the air.

'Hi.'

'You look...' he frowned at her tailored navy skirt and white silk blouse '...very workmanlike.'

'Thank you.' She smiled uncertainly. 'And you look...' she considered the deep blue shorts and blazing multicoloured shirt '...casual—ish.'

'Thanks. The shirt's a bit off the wall.' He shrugged. 'Bought it in South Africa a few years back. Never thought we'd have the weather here to wear it again.'

'South Africa?'

'My folks are there. Cape Town.'

'You didn't mention it before,' she said, sitting at the table.

'You've never asked.'

He was right. She hadn't. 'What do they do?'

He rapped the pan loudly with a spatula. 'Dad's an engineer. Building dams and changing the course of rivers. Mum's an osteopath.'

'Ah. So that's where it comes from.'

'If you mean, my passion for complementary medicine, yes. I guess.'

She leaned her elbows on the table, her eyes mesmerised by the shirt. He did a little trick with the spatula, turning the omelette upside down.

'Clever clogs.'

'Want some? It started as an omelette, but the way things are going, it'll be scrambled.'

'I'll go for the coffee, if that's OK?'

'Safe option,' he agreed, and nodded to the pot on the table. 'It's freshly percolated. Toast's coming up.'

'Oh, don't bother with toast.'

'No trouble.' He dropped two slices of bread into the toaster. Spooning the concoction from the pan, he grimaced. 'Ouch, that's hot.' He ran his tongue over his lips. 'The penalty for showing off.'

She laughed. 'Were you?'

'Of course. Only you didn't say how good it looked—me and the cooking bit.'

She pulled a face. 'I...*think* I'm impressed.'

He gave her a wry smile. 'Reserving judgement, eh? Sensible lady.' Cas turned sharply at the strong smell of burnt toast. 'Will crisps do?' he asked hopefully as he placed the remains in front of her. '*Very* thin crisps.' Under the shock of black hair, she met two apologetic brown eyes that sent her stomach into freefall.

'Is there any reason why you're cooking?' she managed. 'And wearing beach wear?'

'Several.' He sat down beside her and stuck a fork into the eggs.

'Which are?'

'The first—and most obvious—is that the cupboard is empty. It was eggs or the bottom of the cornflakes packet. There wasn't much contest really.'

'And the second?' she asked curiously.

'The second is that it's Tuesday.' He stopped and looked at her. 'And *this* Tuesday morning there's no surgery. Remember? No one loves us. There's a blank page in the book.'

'Tuesday?' she repeated dazedly. 'Oh, flip!'

'Flip's pretty pathetic,' he commented—just—with a full mouth. 'Try something more colourful.'

'I was on autopilot,' she defended, annoyed with herself.

He pushed the empty plate away and massaged his ribs. 'Fancy that. You waking up on autopilot. Me cooking eggs and burnt toast. Sad souls aren't we, without an agenda?'

Abbie tried to ignore the teasing in his eyes and the soft, amused lilt in his voice. 'What about the Dunnings?' she asked. 'We should call, don't you think?'

'*We?*'

'Well, one of us.' She shrugged.

'They'll ring if there's trouble.'

'So you think we should just sit tight?' she asked stupidly.

'Why not? I'll give the hospital a bell, though. Find out how Josie is.' He pulled the toast, which she hadn't dared try, towards him. 'After I've finished this fabulous breakfast which I've been slaving over since the crack of dawn.'

But it wasn't the crack of dawn Abbie was thinking about as, peering at her thoughtfully, Cas broke the toast with supple fingers and crunched them slowly. It was last night that was still on her mind. And what happened on the stairs.

Wishing it could happen all over again.

But Abbie had to think of the future and by Wednesday she'd made a decision. The house had to go on the market. Renting it out wasn't an option. Too much hassle. Besides, it would cost a fortune to make it habitable. There wasn't time for that. And, besides, she had to make a clean break. If she ever came back to England, she'd start afresh.

So on Wednesday afternoon she went to the property agents in Tilly and did the deed. It was a lovely old house, she told them. A family house that had doubled as a country practice for over forty years. A nice young family would like it. The surgery could be turned into a lounge, the office and waiting room knocked into one gorgeous, sun-filled reception room.

Renovated and loved, it would be transformed. She didn't know what central heating cost these days. Or a new roof. And the tiny little black insects that hatched each spring and skittered over the floorboards—even they could be persuaded to leave.

Oh, yes, someone somewhere would fall in love with it.

'I'll be here until September,' she told them decisively. 'In September I go back to the States.'

On Friday afternoon, she called at the Dunnings'. Cas had visited during the week and said Sue and Marjorie were coping. They were. Just. Though Abbie suspected it wouldn't be long before sparks flew.

Abbie had no calls afterwards and decided to drive to the hospital. When she arrived, she found Bob sitting with Josie in a side ward. Though Josie bravely said she felt better, it was clear she wasn't.

'She's having physio for her arm and leg,' Bob told Abbie. 'And speech therapy. She'll soon be back to her old self.'

Abbie wondered if he had come to terms with his wife's ill health. He had leaned on her for so many years, as had all the family.

It was for once, Bob who spoke, regaling Abbie and Josie with stories of Marjorie's attempts to organise the household. Abbie left when the tea trolley arrived and made her way out of the hospital. To her surprise she saw Reggie Donaldson, the local auctioneer, sitting in Reception. He was mopping his forehead and his collar and tie were undone as he blinked the sweat from his eyes.

'I'm in a terrible state,' he admitted. 'I'm trying to calm down before I call a taxi.'

'What happened?' Abbie asked as she sat beside him.

'I came to have my throat examined. The doctor told me to stick out my tongue. Then he put this funny kind of mirror down my throat and said my larynx would be reflected in the lamp on his head.'

'Yes, it's called an indirect laryngoscopy.' Abbie nodded. 'It shouldn't have been too uncomfortable.'

'It wasn't,' Reggie agreed. 'But I got a panic attack and couldn't breathe. So the doctor had to stop. Well, he had to stop a lot of times, really. I feel ashamed of myself. But I don't seem to have any control over it.'

'Did he manage to complete the examination?' Abbie asked.

Reggie shook his head. 'I felt as though I was wasting his time.'

'Come on, I'll drive you home,' Abbie offered, and Reggie looked relieved.

When they arrived at the car Reggie climbed in and let out a long sigh. 'What a day! I wish I'd taken Dr Darke's advice. But until now I didn't realise what a problem I had.'

'What did he suggest?' Abbie asked curiously.

'He told me people hyperventilate when a panic attack happens. He said I should take preventative measures, something relaxing like yoga. Well, fancy telling an auctioneer that! But my wife tore me off a strip and said I should have listened to him.'

'Isn't it worth a try?' Abbie suggested as they arrived at Reggie's cottage. 'You've got nothing to lose.'

Reggie sighed as he opened the door. 'I suppose I haven't. Anyway, thanks for the lift. And I'll have a think about that yoga business.'

Abbie couldn't see Reggie voluntarily turning up at a yoga session. But, then again, it depended how desperate he was. Clearly this last little episode had shaken him.

She arrived back at the surgery, but Cas was nowhere to be found. The four-wheel-drive was by the garage so he must be home, she concluded. A little later she was upstairs, about to change her clothes, when she saw movement in the field next door.

From her window she could see Cas talking to another man, who was dressed in a suit and carrying a briefcase. They were deep in discussion, their attention on the half-completed building. Abbie let her eyes linger for a while on Cas's bronzed shoulders under a chest-hugging white vest and long, powerful legs clad in jeans. He looked relaxed and completely at home in the environment, and it struck her how much hard work he must have put into the polyclinic.

With a gesture that always gave her a tiny shiver, he scooped back his hair with the palm of his hand and the sun gleamed on the thick black pelt. It flopped back into a stubborn wave over his forehead and the unconscious shake he gave caused it to fall heavily down to the nape of his neck.

He pointed a muscular arm towards the second storey and the man with the briefcase nodded slowly. A crane was in place on the other side and it was lowering a wooden beam into the heart of the structure. For the first time Abbie found herself thinking the building might not look so bad after all.

Her gaze returned to the long, broad-shouldered back, the dark, wild hair and the gleam of supple muscle in the afternoon sun.

At that moment Cas turned and glanced up-ward. She stepped back, but maybe too late. Had he seen her? Felt her eyes on him? A shiver of awareness went through her.

Well, he'd said he could read her thoughts, hadn't he?

*   *   *

A week later, Eve Tredlow's pathology report arrived back. Her blood levels had changed and, as Abbie had expected, her medication needed updating. She called at Eve's and Charlie opened the door.

'Nanna's in the garden,' she said. 'Would you like some tea?'

'Yes, thank you, Charlie.'

The girl disappeared and Abbie made her way outside. Eve was resting in a steamer chair, a book on her lap. 'Abbie, this is a lovely surprise.'

Abbie sat beside her and commented on the garden, but Eve looked troubled. 'Sadly, I can't look after it as Frederick used to. He'd be appalled to think how I've let it go.'

'Well, it looks fine to me. Just how I remember it.'

'Yes, of course,' Eve said hesitantly. 'You loved Jane's swing, didn't you? Unfortunately it wasn't safe and I had to have it taken down.' The older woman's face was distracted and Abbie guessed she was recalling her daughter.

Just then Charlie appeared with a tray of tea. She sat beside Abbie on the bench and, as she moved to pour the tea, Abbie caught a faint aroma. She knew at once that this was what had previously caught her attention, though she was

at a loss to think why she hadn't previously iden-
tified it.

She was now certain the smell was marijuana
and as she did her best to reassure Eve about her
medication, she wondered if Eve was aware of
Charlie's habit.

'So, hopefully, no more dizzy spells,' she
ended, then glanced at Charlie. 'Are you enjoy-
ing your stay?'

'Yes,' Charlie said, glancing at her grandmother.

'She's going back to London tonight,' Eve
said quietly.

'Just until tomorrow, Nanna. I need to fetch
some of my things.'

'Charlie, dear…' Eve hesitated. 'Would you
mind making me a sandwich? I feel rather hungry now.'

'I told you to have some breakfast, Nanna.
What would you like? Cheese or ham?'

'Whatever is easiest,' Eve replied, and didn't
speak again until Charlie was out of sight.
'Abbie, I'm worried about Charlie.'

'Why?' Abbie asked.

'She's so restless. And though she says she's
happy here, these little trips back home keep
worrying me. You see, my son-in-law and his
wife are away for the summer, and Charlie's

alone in that big house in London. I don't know if Stuart would be too pleased about the situation.'

'How often does Charlie go home?'

'Last week and a fortnight before that. She's always in a better frame of mind when she comes back. I'm worried that, well, it's really too depressing here for her. She needs something to occupy her mind.'

Abbie felt sorry for Eve. She wasn't in the best of health and was struggling to do her family a good turn. If Charlie was smoking marijuana it was possible she was returning to London for supplies. However, Abbie didn't want to upset the elderly lady by mentioning it. 'Do you think Charlie would like to come in to the surgery for a few hours?' she asked. 'The phone has its moments and there's a fair bit of filing to do.'

'Oh, Abbie, that would be wonderful.'

When Charlie returned with Eve's sandwich, Abbie repeated her suggestion. The girl seemed vaguely interested and the arrangement was made that Charlie should come in the following Monday.

A bright idea that now had to be explained to Cas, Abbie reflected thoughtfully as she drove home. What could she achieve by Charlie coming to the surgery? Cas hadn't thought help in the office was necessary and, really, it wasn't. Not with the flow of patients reduced to such low numbers.

But she had to try and help, try to persuade Charlie to have more sense.

Abbie rolled her eyes and sighed. She knew from experience that Charlie would resent the intrusion. The girl was eighteen. Old enough to vote, old enough to marry.

But certainly not old enough to handle the emotions that seemed to be threatening the family's happiness.

'Sunday's coming up,' Cas said as they sat in the surgery. 'What if I suggested something?'

'Depends,' she murmured. 'On what the something is.'

He leant forward, his tanned forearms resting on the table, one finger slowly circling the top of an empty mug. 'A little diversion.' He shrugged as his dark eyes flickered up and trapped hers. 'Greg's going to be on call on Sunday so we shan't be needed here. Let's drive along the coast, get some sun and fresh air.'

Abbie wondered if now was the time to mention Charlie as a sort of mutual swap. But she didn't think it would go down too well. And it was always possible that Charlie would change her mind.

'We'll eat out. Make a day of it,' he coaxed. 'Take our swimming gear.'

A day away from it all sounded wonderful, and she was on the point of agreeing when he spoke again.

'Abbie?'

'So there is a catch.' She grinned, arching an eyebrow.

'I...' He hesitated. 'I want to thank you for spurring Reggie Donaldson into action. I don't know what you said to him, but he's doing something positive about his panic attacks.'

'Is he?'

'He phoned this morning,' Cas told her with a wry smile. 'Said he's decided to go with his wife to a yoga class.'

Abbie laughed softly. 'Good on Reggie.'

'No,' Cas said quietly. 'Good on you.'

Abbie knew every curve and bend of the Somerset cliffs. Or so she'd thought. Until Cas grabbed her hand tightly, pulled her along a slope of unfamiliar gravel. Before she knew it, they were tumbling down the rocky path to the beach, her auburn curls flying behind her in the breeze.

They were breathless by the time they stopped and Abbie sank down onto a boulder, her green eyes sparkling as she stretched out her legs and wiggled her toes in the sand. 'It's beautiful,' she murmured in amazement. 'I'm certain this place wasn't here before.' She gazed out over the ocean, as blue as a bluebell. The salt washed up into her nose and she gulped down the air, lifting her face to the sun. 'How did you find it?'

'Luck.' He shrugged, sinking down beside her. 'They did a lot of restructuring last year because of the erosion. That's why you didn't recognise it. They're making the gravel slope into a proper path.'

'I remember this cove.' Abbie leaned forward to perch her head on her hands. 'You couldn't get down to it. The cliffs were too steep.'

'Guess nature did it of her own accord,' Cas said, and stretched his arms.

She glanced under her lashes and took a breath. A controlled breath that almost went wrong as she let her eyes drink in the sleek, smooth lines of his beautiful body. His broad shoulders gave him a perfect balance as he stood and brushed the sand from his shorts.

Short shorts, Abbie thought lustfully as her eye traced the masculine curve of neat bottom, tanned thighs and unending legs. Tiny black hairs danced over his skin as it glistened in the bright sun. And she tugged back her eyes, feeling suddenly self-conscious of her tiny frame.

Enviable, she had been told by her friends, though she had never been convinced. A waist too tiny to fit into regular sizes and breasts that were far from a problem. Light and lithe, she had loved cross-country. Nothing outstanding in the sprinting stakes, too slight to be really fast, but she had stamina.

LA had suited her perfectly. Jogging around the bay and through the clean and lovely streets in the early mornings and then down to the park to stare at the sea, glistening under heavy clouds of heat haze.

LA, where she'd first met Jon Kirk, the doctor who had changed her life. And now that there were no emotional ties between them, she knew it had been for the better. Abbie had a fleeting picture of him—a slim, wiry man in his forties, well preserved and charming and totally and utterly dedicated.

'Swim?' Cas asked, and Abbie came back to the present with a little start.

'Is there somewhere we can leave our things?' She narrowed her eyes along the tiny stretch of sand and rock pools.

'Here…to the right. Hold on.'

She slid her fingers into his palm and they picked their way over the rocks beneath the cliff face. He turned and grinned, white teeth sparkling under the sudden slash of smile. 'It's OK. I checked with the coastguard. The tide's on its way out.'

She wondered when he had checked. Before they'd driven here after he'd made the suggestion in the kitchen? Or before she'd come down to breakfast? In which case…she smiled as she climbed over the rocks…in which case it was more than breakfast that had been stage-managed.

'Like it?' They stood at the entrance to a cave, not large by normal cave standards, but big enough for two. Smooth grey rocks and shiny green veins of seaweed glistened as the sun spread its fingers inside and lit up the cavern. 'We can leave our things here,' he suggested, taking her backpack and his. 'Then we'll go round to the beach. The swimming's safe there.'

'Have you been here before?' she asked casually. A knot of something very like jealousy tightened round her ribs. Had he come here with the girlfriend Howard had spoken of? Found this cave, this magical place, and stood gazing out over the sea? Had he looked at her in the same way and held her hand, too?

'Once or twice.' He frowned at her T-shirt and shorts. 'Are you swimming fully clad?'

She ignored the insult and rolled off her T-shirt. She was wearing her bikini, a pale blue one, and she unzipped her shorts and threw them on the pile as his eyes conveyed his thoughts.

'What did you expect?' She grinned. 'Thermals?'

Just then a crash of waves sent a flock of seagulls into the air. 'I've learned to expect the unexpected,' he muttered as he propelled her before him and out into the bright sunlight. 'And I've not been disappointed. So far.'

The sea was cold but Abbie loved every moment. Cas swam ahead of her, his long brown body a snake of light in the water. She followed at a crawl, but in the deeper water she dived, pulling back against the current.

Under the surface it was silent and dark. Though she tried to clear her vision, a field of seaweed surrounded the beach. She pushed up, breaking the surface, and suddenly he was beside her, tossing back his wet black hair.

'You're a strong swimmer,' he shouted, and she laughed, her wet curls threaded with seaweed.

'Race you back,' she called.

'You're on.'

It was a long, hard slog against the current. She'd known it would be, striking out against the tide and conserving her energy for the last haul. She knew she wouldn't win—but it was close and when they reached the cove the waves swept them in gently to the soft, shingle beach.

They lay in the sun, recovering, as the surf brushed languidly over the rocks. 'I'd forgotten just how lovely it is,' she said breathlessly as she gazed out to sea.

'Yes,' he murmured. 'Lovelier every time I look.'

There was a note in his voice she didn't recognise, and as she turned back she sensed that he hadn't been looking at the sea. But gazing at her.

CHAPTER SEVEN

SHE hadn't been mistaken, or had she? There had been desire in Cas's eyes and her heart had somersaulted.

The same look she had seen the night he'd kissed her. A look that had reached inside to her soul. A look that could have been followed by his touch and the warm urgency of his mouth on hers...

And pigs might fly, Abbie corrected herself as she watched him roll back on the sand as if she'd given him an electric shock. He gave a growl of discontent at the sky, which had admittedly clouded over, and he lobbed a bit of driftwood into the sea.

'We're not leaving, are we?' she called, sitting up.

'Want to swim again?' He lifted his hand to his brow to gaze back at her. 'If you do, we'd better hurry. The weather's changing.'

She stood up and brushed the sand from her bikini. 'Wait for me, then.'

They did swim again. But he didn't wait. He struck out, head down and legs powering beneath the surface. She let him disappear and ignored the fierce departure that appeared to denote boredom.

She tried to enjoy a lazy swim but headed back to the cave as solid little marbles of rain fell from the sky. She dried herself quickly, happy to have brought a thick, chunky sweater to wear over her shorts. Once warm, she sat on a rock and tried to dislodge the seaweed from her hair.

He arrived then, splashing noisily into the cave. And padded around, presumably searching for his towel.

'I put it up here to keep dry.' She reached up to a dry ledge and pulled it down.

No 'thank you'—just a grunt as his head disappeared in the folds.

'Good swim?' she asked hopefully.

'Great,' he rasped, burying his head in the towel once more.

'Fine.' Abbie waited, thinking he might surface with a smile. But he didn't. He turned his back, and, trying to ignore the long, tanned expanse of wet skin, she stood at the entrance. 'See you on the beach.'

He muttered what she thought was an affirmative and she left him to it. Ten minutes later he joined her on the sand where she had been sitting, idly waiting for a downpour.

'Hungry?' he said, slinging his sports bag over his shoulder. His wet hair was combed back and he wore a light sweater over his shorts. And he looked a fraction less disgruntled, she decided. But only a fraction.

'Ravenous.'

'There's a beach café a couple of miles along the road.' He looked at his watch and added shortly, 'Or do you want to go home and change first?'

It would have been nice to go home and shower, she thought, but the emphasis was on the café. And, in Cas's present mood, a night out seemed as likely as winning the lottery.

'The café will do,' she said, and hoped that by the time he'd eaten and satisfied the man inside him she would have the courage to tell him about Charlie.

The café was closed for renovations. Then the sky opened up, so that the road in front of them became a river.

'I suppose we'd better go home,' she said, dully acknowledging defeat.

'I'll stop for a take-away.' He pulled up in Tilly at the newly opened Chinese restaurant. Despite looking nearly drowned when he returned, the thought—or smell—of the food seemed to cheer him.

They ate in the kitchen with the food spread over the table. Rain hurtled against the windows, reminding Abbie how fickle the weather could be. But the room was cosy and the food was wonderful. And Cas's mood had improved.

Food, or the lack of it, she assumed, had been the culprit.

The one fly in the ointment was the telephone. It hadn't rung. Neither Eve nor Charlie had left a message to say that tomorrow wasn't such a good idea after all.

When it did ring, Abbie was the first to answer it. She heard the crackle of static—no doubt, the storm—and then a man's voice.

'Abbie, it's me. Can you hear me OK?'

'Jon?' she said in surprise.

'How are you?'

'I'm fine.'

'Have you any plans for the last week in July?'

'July?' She stared at the desk. 'No…well, I don't know—'

'Because I'm coming over.'

'You're coming to England?' she asked stupidly.

'Uh-huh. I'm on the campaign trail—for the clinic. We'll be doing the UK—radio, TV, the works. I'd like to see you, Abbie. Could we get together?'

'Jon, I'd like to, but—'

'Great. I'll be in touch. See you soon, honey.'

The line went dead and she slowly replaced the phone. Jon Kirk, her trainer in the States, was coming to England. He hadn't mentioned the trip when she'd been making plans after the funeral. But, then, she shouldn't be surprised. He was a dynamic man. And totally committed to the work he did, promoting his work whenever and wherever he could.

'It was for you?' a voice said, and Abbie turned to find Cas staring at her.

'Yes.' She nodded. 'Jon Kirk. A doctor I work for in the States.' Abbie wondered how long Cas had been standing there.

'And this…Jon Kirk is coming to England,' Cas said dryly.

'You heard?'

'I thought…' he shrugged '…that it might be Greg.'

'Well, it wasn't Greg. It was Jon. And he's arriving in July.'

'Ah…' He nodded slowly. 'I see.'

What did he see? she wondered. It was as though Cas was inferring Jon was more to her than an employer—perhaps a boyfriend. 'He's promoting the clinic—' she felt impelled to add, but he cut her off with a short, dry laugh.

'Promoting? Surely that's unnecessary. Cosmetic surgery is splashed daily over every glossy magazine on God's earth.'

Abbie narrowed her eyes and stood up. Her intention to explain that Jon Kirk was her employer and nothing more was swiftly forgotten. If Cas insisted on being objectionable, then she would give him something to be objectionable about. 'Do you enjoy listening to other people's conversations?' she demanded crisply.

'Only when I feel at a disadvantage,' he informed her coolly. 'You see, I happen to care about what goes on under this roof. At least, as long as I'm living under it. Which, fortunately, I won't be for much longer.'

'Really?' Abbie retorted, folding her arms. 'Thank you for the good news.'

'But until that day,' he continued, 'I'd like to be consulted before an eighteen-year-old unqualified teenager turns up on the doorstep who'll, no doubt, need supervision every damn second she's here.' He thrust a piece of paper in her hand. '*This* is obviously meant for you. It was on the mat.'

Abbie peered at the two sentences scrawled across Eve's headed lavender-coloured notepaper.

'I'll arrive for work at nine o'clock, if that's OK. Could you ring Nanna, if it isn't? Charlie.'

Abbie looked up to explain, but he'd disappeared.

Charlie must have called whilst they'd been at the beach, she realised. In their rush to eat, neither of them had spotted the note. Not until Cas had lurked in the hall, listening to a conversation that was supposed to be private!

A knife could have cut the atmosphere next morning.

'Eve was upset,' Abbie tried to explain over the cornflakes. 'Charlie is at a loose end, so I just suggested she do some filing for us. We are in a muddle in the office.'

'Tell me about it,' Cas muttered grimly. 'Abbie, we aren't a nannying service.'

'Charlie isn't irresponsible,' Abbie protested.

'And she isn't qualified to work in a medical practice either.'

Abbie coloured. 'There's something else I have to tell you.'

He looked at her, horror-stricken. 'Now what?'

'I realised what's wrong with Charlie.' She paused. 'She's smoking.'

'Cigarettes?'

'No, marijuana.'

'Oh, great!' He threw his head back and made a sound through his teeth like an electric saw. 'Just what we need.'

'No, we don't need it at all, I agree,' Abbie replied defensively. 'But it's Charlie's needs that count, too.'

'And you're an authority on adolescent psychology, are you?' he boomed.

She gave up then. And waited.

They sat in silence until he stuck his spoon into his uneaten cornflakes and stood up. 'As of this moment, the girl is your responsibility,' he told her firmly. 'You're in surgery this morning. So it's down to you…and if…' he spluttered, as though words were beyond him. But obviously finding none to fit, he turned angrily on his heel and marched out.

Abbie sat listening to the clatter going on in the office. When the front door closed and Cas had gone off on his calls, Abbie breathed out. Long and slowly.

Five minutes later, she was in the office. Most of the paperwork was NHS correspondence and letters. It would take hours to go through and file. And there was more in the cupboard under the stairs. By the time she had loaded it all onto the desk, Charlie was ringing the doorbell.

The girl looked pale under her braided dark hair, but she smiled and Abbie took her into the office and sat her down. 'All this stuff needs to be sorted alphabetically and put in the file there.'

'No problem.' Charlie shrugged. 'And by the way, I type.'

'Do you? Great. Can you use a computer?'

Charlie nodded and Abbie went off to make a coffee. She returned to find Charlie carefully sorting out the mountain of paperwork and placed the mug on the desk.

'I'm in surgery this morning, just across the hall,' she said. 'The patients wait in that little room to the left. Don't worry if you don't see any. We're winding down before we close.'

Charlie looked up then. 'Are you?'

Abbie nodded. 'Dr Darke is building a poly-clinic next door. Haven't you seen it going up?'

Charlie shrugged. 'No. What's a polyclinic?'

'A health centre of traditional and comple-mentary medicine.'

'Oh, cool.'

Abbie smiled. 'Yes, it has a ring to it, doesn't it?'

Charlie grinned. 'What about the phone?'

'If it's a patient wanting an appointment, here's the book.' Abbie slid it across the desk. 'If it's a call, one of us will go—probably this afternoon, unless it's an emergency. Press this button if you want to talk to me on the extension.'

'OK.' Charlie nodded and Abbie left her, wondering if she would regret not heeding Cas's warning about supervising her. Well, she couldn't have her in with the patients. And she couldn't sit with her in the office all morning. So she would just have to pop in every now and then.

As only three patients turned up that morning, it was easy enough. And when Cas returned he found them together in the office.

'Hello,' he said gruffly.

'Hello, Dr Darke,' Charlie said pleasantly, and resumed her filing.

'Is there a coffee going?' he asked, and Abbie smiled sweetly.

'It's just percolated. Help yourself.'

She had the satisfaction of seeing the look of surprise on his face as she settled back in her seat at the desk. When he had gone, she glanced at Charlie. Cas's abruptness seemed to have passed unnoticed.

Abbie smiled to herself.

Maybe everything was going to work out nicely after all.

*   *   *

By July, the estate agents had started to show people round. Mostly speculators. All with their own ideas of what a decent-sized country house with a doctor's surgery included could be turned into. A smallholding, a guest house, a holiday home. No one wanted it for a family. Everyone said the roof and the central heating would cost the earth. And as for the woodworm...!

Abbie decided, after the fifth grand tour, she would make herself scarce and allow the agents to do their job. It was an arrangement that worked well, provided they gave her the date and time. She asked them not to plan any tours until after morning surgery, when the surgery and waiting room would be clear of patients.

One hot Friday morning, Abbie returned from her calls to discover a red car parked in front of the office window. It was eleven thirty and Cas's surgery should have been over, Abbie thought as she approached the open front door.

'Charlie?' Abbie glanced in the office. Empty. Perhaps Cas had sent her home? But then she saw the little string bag that Charlie always hung over her chair.

To Abbie's surprise, both the waiting room and surgery were empty. Then a rattle came from the kitchen. Charlie was there, arranging cups and saucers on a tray.

'Hi.' Abbie smiled.

'You've got a visitor.' Charlie nodded to the garden. 'I think it might be someone to look at the house, though Dr Darke didn't say. He asked me just to make some tea.'

'The agents must have sent someone,' Abbie sighed, wondering why they hadn't phoned her first. 'Put another cup on for me, would you, Charlie? Oh—and how's the computer?'

'Cool,' Charlie said, grinning.

'Really?'

'Yeah.'

Charlie certainly wasted few words, Abbie reflected as she left her case in the surgery. She had been at the surgery for two weeks now and on the whole seemed happy enough.

Even Cas had been forced to agree that the arrangement was working well. Charlie had asked him to set up the computer, which had been gathering dust. She had done an IT course at college and was, as she said, computer friendly.

Cas had been doubtful. But that, Abbie had decided, was because he didn't welcome the time consumed in setting up the machine. He'd spent a whole evening with the manual before he'd booted it up successfully, complaining that if

Charlie had been fantasising about her skills, the effort would have been for nothing.

'What were you going to do with it anyway?' Abbie had asked, as he'd wrestled with an octopus of cables. 'It couldn't sit in that box for ever.'

'It wouldn't have,' he'd replied, and had thrust the last plug into the back. 'It was meant for next door.'

'Well, you'll be all set up beforehand, won't you?' she'd replied smartly.

Not that she'd got a response. All he'd done had been to mutter under his breath about taking the whole lot to pieces again.

The following morning, Charlie had switched on and sailed away.

'She does know how to use it,' Cas had conceded as they stood in surgery, examining a perfectly printed letter that Charlie had fashioned.

'And the office is tidy and all the rubbish is dumped and the important stuff filed,' Abbie had added meaningfully. 'Charlie really seems to like the work.'

'Don't count your braids.' He'd grinned, referring to Charlie's wayward hairstyle, and had departed to check on her again.

Abbie went in search of Cas and the visitors and gave in to gloating. It was just a small gloat, but she felt she deserved it. Taking on Charlie had been a good move. And there had been no smoking marijuana. At least not at work. And Charlie hadn't done any of her disappearing tricks.

Even Cas seemed less disgruntled, back to his old self. Though she was beginning to wonder what his old self—or *real* self, really was. It was undoubtedly a good sign that he'd asked Charlie to make tea.

She wondered who the visitor was. Cas was obviously doing his best to impress. Pausing in the downstairs cloakroom, she scrutinised her appearance. Casual blouse and linen trousers—yes, they'd do. Hair, as usual, an array of wilful auburn curls but, all things being equal, acceptable. Her freckles, thankfully, had receded into her tan. And her eyes had lost their tired little arrows of grief.

A few minutes later she was outside, following the path around the side of the house. The air was deliciously sultry. She breathed it in like a fine old wine. A day on which anything was possible, she thought wistfully as she rounded the hedge by the field, over which she could hear hammering and sawing.

But even the workmen's noise added to her well-being. A euphoria that lasted right up until she rounded the privet and paused, as she found herself staring at the two figures sitting on the bench.

Cas laughed softly, a deep, rich sound that Abbie hadn't heard for days. The young blonde woman sitting beside him reached out and brushed something invisible from his shirt. Her long fingers trailed along the ridge of his arm. Slowly, provocatively, until Abbie thought she was going to pass out, waiting for them to fall away.

Finally they did and Abbie stepped back behind the hedge. They hadn't seen her, she realised, despite blundering in on their romantic interlude. They seemed far too wrapped up in each other to notice anything else, she decided as she retraced her steps to the house. The next thing she knew she was back in the cloakroom.

Trying to think what she should do next.

What she had to do next, of course, was exactly what she didn't want to do. Because Charlie had put three cups on the tray. And unless she could dredge up a cast-iron excuse as to why she'd failed to materialise, she was going to have to walk out there and introduce herself.

She knew who the visitor was now.

Howard Bailey had spoken of Cas's girlfriend who, it seemed, her mind had conveniently forgotten for the last two months. What was it Howard had said? She'd upset Ben Armitage and scared the life out of the poor old biddy in the chemist.

Abbie took a hopeful glance in the mirror. She'd looked fine ten minutes ago, now she looked dull and uninteresting.

A knot twisted unhelpfully in her stomach.

Surely she wasn't jealous?

'No way,' she assured her reflection, ignoring the evasive glint of deep, shifting green in her eyes. Why on earth should she be? Though she had to admit the packaging was gorgeous—a designer suit that clung like a second skin and tweaked at all the strategic points.

However, she must face the enemy.

'Enemy?' Abbie gasped, staring into the mirror. 'What on earth am I thinking?' she asked incredulously. 'I don't even know the woman.'

Abbie crept out of the cloakroom and bumped straight into Charlie.

She smiled guiltily. 'Tea all done?'

Charlie nodded. 'Dr Darke wanted to know where you were.'

'Oh, did he?' she asked innocently.

'I told him you were in the cloakroom.'

'Fine,' Abbie sighed, defeated. And sloped off toward the garden. When she turned the hedge, Cas saw her this time.

'Abbie,' he called, waving her over.

'Hello.'

'Abbie, this is a friend of mine from London. Venetia, meet Abbie.'

Venetia. Yes, of course, it would be Venetia. Or Fenella. Or Annabelle. The gorgeous ivory designer suit slithered into a crease-free sheath as the young woman sat forward. 'Hello, Abbie.'

'Venetia works in the City,' Cas continued brightly. 'In marketing.'

'How interesting.'

'That last time I came down to the sticks,' Venetia cooed, 'you were in the States.'

Abbie plastered on a sweet smile. 'I heard you met a few of the locals. Ben Armitage—and the lady in the chemist?'

'Oh, yes,' Venetia agreed vaguely. 'A rather quarrelsome little woman and very bad-tempered horse owner.' Venetia's lashes flickered at the unpleasant memory.

'Venetia's staying for the weekend,' Cas said quickly, slanting a warning frown in Abbie's direction. 'The Crow is pretty basic, so I thought we'd try the King's Head.'

'Why not?' Abbie shrugged.

'Well, I was hoping—' Venetia began, but Cas cut her off with a heart-stopping smile.

'I thought we could meet for dinner tomorrow,' he said, adding hurriedly, 'And you must come, too, Abbie.'

'Yes,' Venetia agreed with all the warmth of an iceberg.

'Well, maybe.' Abbie gestured wildly to the house. 'Anyway, must dash. I'm giving Charlie a lift home.'

'The little girl in the office with the funny hair? What an odd little person she is,' Venetia tinkled, and Abbie fought the urge to strangle her.

She dragged up a smile instead. 'I'll be here this afternoon if you two want to escape.'

Inside the house, Abbie found Charlie in the office. 'Hop in the car,' she told her. 'I'll give you a lift home.'

'It's early yet.' Charlie looked surprised.

'It's too nice to be in. And, besides, I'm going your way.'

'OK.' Charlie shrugged and switched off the computer.

Abbie drove to the Tredlows' with determination. She had no intention of watching Venetia and Cas together and even less inclination to meet them for dinner. Cas was welcome to indulge in Venetia's company, she told herself indifferently. But the thought of Venetia's long and lovely body curled in Cas's arms made her feel a touch malevolent.

Though why it should was a mystery…

Or was it?

CHAPTER EIGHT

ABBIE stopped to speak with Eve who was in good spirits. The change in her medication had helped, and when Charlie was out of earshot she said that her granddaughter seemed more settled now she had something to do.

Abbie drove back to Tilly by the cliff road. It was a glorious Friday afternoon and the blue of the ocean soothed her. Seeing Venetia and Cas together had given her a shock. She tried thinking logically. Cas was entitled to do what he liked. See whom he liked. And it was pointless to get in a state about it.

'I'm not,' Abbie told herself as she drove. 'That's ridiculous.'

Exactly.

'So go home now and don't let him see that he's upset you.'

Well, he hasn't.

By the time Abbie got back to the surgery, the jazzy sports car had gone. But so had Cas's vehicle. He was probably out with her—investigating the bedrooms at the King's Head. Abbie was just thankful he hadn't suggested she stay here.

Waking up to Venetia gliding through the house wouldn't have been her idea of fun. And anyway, none of the other bedrooms had been aired. Which, she thought grumpily, was beside the point. Because she would be sleeping in Cas's, wouldn't she?

The workmen next door were just finishing, driving out onto the road in clouds of dust. Eager to be away. Reluctant to admit that weekend yawned ahead, Abbie changed into shorts and a loose shirt. Except for tomorrow night. An invitation that she was definitely going to refuse.

'No way am I playing gooseberry,' she vowed as she made a long, cool drink and took it into the garden.

Sitting on the bench and sipping earnestly, she found herself giving far more thought to the subject than she liked. Cas had probably forgotten he'd suggested the meal, anyway. And even if he hadn't, she would simply say no. She had some very important things to do.

'Like what?' Abbie demanded, as she swung her legs up onto the bench and closed her eyes to think.

'Like clearing the house,' she answered. There was stuff hidden in the house from decades past. All her things and her parents' furniture.

Most of it was valueless. Some pieces she could put into store. Others she'd have to find homes for. Then there were Dad's books. Dozens of them, stuffed on shelves and in cupboards. She'd have to go through each one and decide its fate.

'And Mum's piano,' she sighed softly, 'though goodness knows it hasn't been played in years—'

'What hasn't?' a voice asked, and Abbie jumped.

She blinked. Cas's silhouette sent her heart skyrocketing. 'Oh, it's you.'

'Yes, only me,' he said ruefully, and folded up his long body on the steamer chair beside her bench.

'I was thinking aloud,' she mumbled, wondering how long he had been watching her.

'Like someone real to think out loud to?'

'I was just going in,' she lied, and was about to lower her legs to stand when he shook his head.

'Don't move. You look so comfortable.' Cas's voice was husky and his eyes slid over her bare legs, like smooth, warm chocolate over her skin. Her heart did a funny kind of sizzle as she watched him lie back and settle himself comfortably.

Not that he looked terribly comfortable. He still wore his white shirt and long dark trousers and wrestled with the top button of the shirt, skewing the tie, giving a little groan of irritation as it refused to budge.

Abbie's eyes flickered down to the well of his throat. It looked soft and exposed with tiny black hairs crowded around the opening of his shirt. She wondered if Venetia's silky blonde hair had been pressed against it as they'd said goodbye.

'You were saying?' he prompted, his eyes closed. 'About pianos?'

'Nothing much. It's just that I don't know what to do with it.'

'Can't it stay where it is?' He wasn't aware of her gaze and she tried to keep her thoughts focused. It wasn't easy when everything about him roared sex appeal. Those long black lashes fanned down on his cheeks, the way he lay on the steamer, his chest rising gently and his long legs casually crossed at the ankles.

'No,' she replied weakly, losing the battle with her thoughts. 'The next owners wouldn't want it.'

'You mean, when the house is sold?'

'Yes,' she replied, and shrugged. 'I'll have to store a few pieces, but the fewer the better.'

'So…you're quite determined to go back?'

'To LA?' She nodded.

'And does this decision have any bearing on Jon Kirk?'

'Jon?' she repeated, frowning. 'Yes…it does, of course…' Looking into his eyes, she realised what he was thinking and added quickly, 'But not in the way—'

'You don't have to explain,' he cut in. Thrusting back his hair with a heavy hand, he glowered at her.

Why was the subject of her return to the States such a sticking point between them? She had always intended to return after settling Dad's affairs. But Cas had started to make her feel guilty about her decision.

'I booked Venetia in at the King's Head,' he told her suddenly. 'And I reserved a table for eight tomorrow evening.'

'Sorry,' Abbie said, deciding it would do no harm to let him think that Jon was her boyfriend. It would make a pleasant change from the topic of Venetia. 'I won't be able to come.'

'What?' He opened his eyes and stared at her. 'You said you'd come this afternoon.'

'I didn't. I said I might.'

'So what happened in between?'

'Just…things,' she replied evasively. 'Besides, there's surgery to cover.'

'No, there isn't. I've already rung Greg. He owes me a favour for standing in last Saturday.' He lifted one dark eyebrow. 'Oh, come on, Abbie. Don't be a stick-in-the-mud.'

'I'm not!' she gasped.

'You are.' He grinned and she bit her lip and hesitated. Just long enough for him to pounce in with, 'That's settled, then—we deserve a good meal. It'll make up for the one we didn't have before.'

A soft little flutter of memory trailed around in her head. The day at the beach and their swim and the take-away which had almost been drenched in the storm. Abbie sighed. There had been only two of them then. And she would have eaten out of newspaper that day and not really noticed.

She gritted her teeth and accepted fate. Perhaps in the next twenty-four hours Venetia might get chickenpox. Or flu. Or hay fever.

Unfair, Abbie Scott, she berated herself, and glanced guiltily at Cas. He sat back and gave her the wildest of smiles. One that left her feeling pathetically spineless.

Abbie stared at the four different outfits thrown over the bed and rolled her eyes.

'Why am I doing this?' she demanded aloud. 'All I had to do was say no. Or thank you but, no, thank you. Or, well—anything, but agree to a gooseberry evening.' She picked up the LA dress, but she'd worn it when she'd come home and Cas would remember. Not, of course, that it mattered. But she wasn't in an LA mood and she didn't feel like the little black suit that she'd worn to the solicitors either.

And the navy blue silk shift? She picked it up and shook out a cloud of dust. It needed cleaning. Then she tried on the long skirt with polka dots. At least a decade out of fashion, it would look staid and frumpy. Everything else she had brought with her was functional. Not dressy.

'Oh, anything will do,' she grumbled, knowing it wouldn't. She'd feel self-conscious all evening and wish that she'd made an effort. Scooping up the lot and pushing them back into their respective compartments, she wondered if it was too late to drive into Tilly.

She shouldn't have taken that walk down to the sea after surgery. Or sat in the garden afterwards, feeling sorry for herself. Now it was five o'clock and no amount of self-pity was going to change the fact she had nothing to wear.

Would she catch that little boutique in the market square open? The new one she'd noticed when she'd been called to Tilly Tearooms? Tonight's meal deserved action, she decided bravely—and flew out of the house.

She caught the sales assistant turning the sign on the door. With breathless apologies, she persuaded her that she was in earnest need. 'Can I try on that?' Abbie pointed to a dress in the window. It looked soft and sexy—if she had the courage to wear it.

She tried it on and decided that if she wore her hair up it would probably do.

'What do you think?' she asked the girl.

'What's it for? A show, or something?'

'No,' Abbie admitted. 'Just dinner. At the King's Head.'

'Oh.' The girl heaved in a consoling breath. 'Well, the colour works. And you're small. You can take the style. As you're so tiny, you wouldn't want anything loose and floppy.'

Loose and floppy, no. But quite so, well, revealing? But the dress did feel gorgeous. As soft as silk—which it probably wasn't but doubled perfectly. Figure-hugging with tiny little straps. Pale green, which reminded her of spring buds and did something wonderful for her eyes.

'I'll take it.'

'You're sure?'

Not quite the response she wanted, but Abbie said she was. She hoped she could find the pretty strappy sandals that would go with it which were buried somewhere at home.

'Good luck at The King's Head,' the girl said as she left.

'Thanks.' Abbie smiled. 'I'll probably need it.'

Luck, she decided, didn't come into it. Not with Venetia to talk to all evening. Though the dress was green, she mused, even if it was the palest, wispiest green. And it made her feel almost lucky. After all, Venetia was only human. And she wasn't going to hurl herself at Cas all through dinner. Or kiss him passionately in front of a full restaurant.

Was she?

Despite minor setbacks, which included the loss and discovery of one strappy pair of sandals and the fight with newly washed hair that flatly refused to be pinned up, by seven-thirty Abbie was dressed.

She felt the girl in the boutique would have been proud of her. The dress clung to her body with a surprising compliance and the high-heeled sandals had been worth rescuing. They gave her those added few inches that would bring her up to Venetia's Adam's apple.

No doubt Venetia would be wearing something sexy and definitely not off the peg. But, then, it was only dinner they all had to struggle through. And even if pangs of envy far greener than the dress she was wearing did knit Abbie's ribs together, she was determined not to let it show.

After all, she had been living in one of the world's trendiest cities for the last two years. And she did know what fashion was all about even if she hadn't had much time to indulge herself.

It hadn't even occurred to her to spend hours trawling through the malls or searching the little shops. Maybe she would have if she'd lived in the fast lane and tried to compete with the beautiful, fashion-conscious women that came into the private hospital where she had first worked.

Abbie gazed in the mirror and sighed. Well, she'd given it her best shot. And it just hadn't worked out. And she wasn't going to think about it now, anyway. There was Venetia to consider.

One slow, studied twirl in the mirror, a generous spray of scent—and she was there. Her hair, the evening's culprit, was holding. Just. She had brushed and twisted her wild and slippery auburn curls into a knot, then enthusiastically stabbed it with a fashion clip. The clip had worked, until she'd moved, when a little ping had preceded an avalanche of auburn waves around her ears.

But she had persevered and succeeded. The clip remained steadfast and the slim, creamy arch of her neck was now exposed to the naked slope of her shoulders and the fragile straps that crossed them.

Finally, her accessories. A small matching bag, a slender gold chain. And a glistening thread of bracelet. No doubt Venetia would look sumptuous. Abbie wondered where Cas had met her. What was their relationship? Close enough to follow him to the ends of the rural earth, Abbie thought as she peeped out of the window and saw Cas walk out of the house.

Her heart did its usual unwieldy lurch as her eyes drank in his tall figure. He was wearing a dark suit—not a dinner suit—something more casual, but absolutely gorgeous. Cut sleekly and favouring his height, it was enough to stir that nasty little jolt of something unpleasant inside her. Obviously Venetia brought out the best in him.

And he'd had his hair cut. It didn't catch his collar any more. Her eyes watched furtively as he unlocked the front door of his vehicle and opened it. For a moment he bent, then slowly withdrew something. Was it a bouquet?

It was.

Her heart raced as she saw the deep scarlet blush of roses under Cellophane. They were tied with a great, shiny red bow. She swallowed, not daring to move. Had he really gone out to buy her roses? He stood still for a moment and Abbie's heart sang with joy.

Then it sank like a stone as he went round to the back of the vehicle, opened the door and lowered the roses inside.

Abbie felt sick.

How could she have been so stupid as to imagine they were for her?

If she hadn't known better, she would have thought the dress had worked. Cas's eyes followed her as she came downstairs and stood uncertainly in the hall.

For a moment they seemed to hover on her hair and then the dress, as though he were looking at a stranger. Then they flashed, very slightly, like a streak of lightning across a brown velvet sky. And Abbie saw them darken, as she had occasionally in the past when they'd seemed almost black.

Then he'd straightened and cleared his throat. 'I haven't seen that dress before,' he muttered in a confused sort of tone. 'Have I?'

Not the best start, she decided as she came to stand beside him. 'No. I bought it today.'

'Ah. So that's where you were after surgery.'

She pushed back a strand of auburn curl from her eyes and fluttered her eyelashes. As she hadn't seen him all day, she found that statement interesting. 'Were you looking for me?' she asked, and wondered if he was staring at her hair for some reason. His eyes were creeping upward and she had the horrible feeling that her careful construction of curls was in danger of collapse.

'Not really. I just didn't see you about the house.'

'Possibly because I went for a walk.' She looked up at him curiously. 'I didn't see you either. I was back at three and sat in the garden.'

'Oh.' He nodded, as his gaze travelled slowly down and seemed to be locked on one shoulder strap which had fallen slightly from her shoulder. 'I was...um...taking Venetia to the hairdresser's.'

A knot of jealousy tightened in her stomach as she thought of the fight she'd had with her own unsatisfactory thatch of curls. Venetia's long, to-

die-for blonde hair had apparently been the un-
swerving focus of a hairdresser all afternoon.

'Lucky Venetia,' Abbie mumbled.

'Yes,' agreed Cas absently, making a stabbing
gesture towards her shoulder. 'You've, um, come
adrift.'

'Oh, my strap,' Abbie huffed, still fighting
with the picture of Venetia and a veil of exquisite
blonde hair.

'Shall I?' Cas's hands were raised and hovering and she nodded vaguely. Why did Cas have
to take Venetia anyway? The only hairdresser
that Tilly possessed was in the high street.
Admittedly at the far end, but walkable.
Especially from the King's Head. It really was…

Abbie felt her thoughts shudder to a halt. His
fingers were fluttering gently over her skin. And
his brows were dragged together in a deep, un-
restful pleat. He was so close she could feel his
breath on her cheek. What was he doing? And
then she felt his fingers brush her skin and she
remembered. He was trying to haul up her strap,
which kept falling over her arm. He gave a little
grunt and tried again. She let him struggle because she enjoyed seeing him at a disadvantage.

And, anyway, she still felt cross.

Cross about Venetia and the hairdresser. Cross
that she'd had to rush out and buy a new dress.

And even crosser at the roses. Those gorgeous, wonderful red roses that he'd slyly removed from the front seat and hidden in the back.

'You're not standing properly,' he complained, his fingers dragging the strap over her shoulder. 'You're slouching. That's why it keeps falling off.'

'I am not.' She stood up straight and he gave a snort.

'There, you see. Perfect.' He stepped back and grinned.

'Aren't we going to be late?' she asked stonily.

She was pleased to see the grin disappear and when he opened the door for her to walk out, she lifted her head. All she had to get through was the next two or maybe three hours.

It couldn't be that difficult, could it?

A question to which she had an immediate answer. She forgot to lower her head as she climbed into the four-wheel-drive. Forgot, because she saw one of the leaves of the roses on the floor.

Incriminating evidence, she thought spitefully just before the impact.

'Ouch!' She fell on the seat.

Cas came round and stared into her face. 'What's wrong?'

'Nothing,' she whimpered through painful tears.

'You bumped your head, didn't you?' he accused. 'It's that stupid thing in your hair.'

Her lips twitched as she glared at him. 'Oh, thank you!'

'You have beautiful hair,' he said. 'Why hide it?'

'I wasn't,' she protested, wondering if he meant it. 'I wore it up especially. For your wretched dinner—which I wish I'd never agreed to.'

'Well, if that's the case,' he snarled, 'we'd better call it off.'

For a moment he stood in furious silence until she heard a little ping and waited for the avalanche. It came, her hair springing wildly from the clip, her auburn curls clustering happily back around her face.

With something close to a smile, he reached out and disentangled the clip. It was hanging at half-mast in her hair and he pulled gently at the nasty little knots. He was right, of course. If she'd wanted to wear it up she could have tied it back with something far less lethal. It was all Venetia's fault, she thought miserably.

'Here.' He thrust the offensive weapon towards her.

'Thank you,' she mumbled, hoping her hair wasn't hanging around her ears like Frankenstein's bride's.

'It's…' he began, thrusting one hand deeply into his pocket and waving the other towards her head, 'it's much better like that. Really. You don't need anything in it. It's beautiful, just the way it is.'

For some reason she wasn't really clear about she wanted to believe he meant it. She had thought she was dressing to compete with Venetia. She didn't want to look a country bumpkin. But when she'd come downstairs and Cas had looked at her with an unreadable expression and hadn't even said the dress looked nice, Venetia's opinion hadn't seemed to matter at all.

'How's the head?' he asked.

'Better,' she said, 'now that it hasn't got so much on top of it.'

He smiled softly. 'So what are we going to do?' He leaned against the car and she felt a shiver go down her spine. 'Cancel?'

'We can't,' Abbie grumbled, swinging her legs into the vehicle. 'Venetia will be waiting.'

He gave her a crooked frown as she closed the door, then went round and jumped in beside her.

It was a good thing his thought-reading mechanism wasn't in progress, she decided as he re-

versed. Venetia now had chickenpox *and* flu—
and was definitely not sociable, or more
importantly, kissable.

Wrong on all four counts, Abbie decided as she
sat at the table and folded and unfolded her napkin. Venetia hadn't a spot in sight, was looking
in the peak of health, was mind-bogglingly sociable. And definitely looked kissable. She had
put something very shiny on her lips and kept
making mewing little sounds that had Cas looking at her with those dark brown eyes. And hanging on every word she uttered.

Abbie, meanwhile, had compressed her napkin
into every shape imaginable whilst listening to
Venetia. And with all due credit to the King's
Head, it had survived the three courses with
amazing elasticity.

'When we first met,' Venetia was saying, looking ravishingly enticing in a deep blue dress that
plunged way beyond belief at the front, 'I didn't
think anyone could cure me. But Caspar was fantastic. He found the problem straight away.'

I'll bet, thought Abbie, throwing a glance at
Cas who seemed unaware that Venetia had been
prattling on for the last hour.

'He said I needed heaps more exercise,'
Venetia continued, batting her long blonde eye-

lashes. 'Being in an office and at meetings all day gives you this awful stress thing. Across your shoulders.'

Abbie knew the feeling. She had it right now. It might go if Venetia could just hurry up and finish that minuscule dessert that she'd been toying with for the last half-hour. Then there would only be coffee to endure.

'So he suggested the gym—which was, of course, where we *really* met. We just sort of bumped into each other the next week.' Venetia stretched across and patted Cas's arm with long, glossy pink fingernails. 'So I suppose it wasn't exactly a coincidence—' She broke off, going pink as she smiled shyly.

'Fate,' Abbie said, and plastered on a smile.

Cas and Venetia stared at her.

'Fate?' she repeated. 'It was fate that brought you together.'

Venetia tinkled laughter. 'Oh, I see what you mean.'

Abbie smiled sweetly. 'And did the exercise help your stress?'

'Oh, yes.' Venetia nodded. 'And it does wonders for the figure. But you've got to have the right exercises. For instance, I don't need to improve here—' Venetia glanced down at her neckline which, Abbie reflected, was hardly an appropriate description for the wisps she was wearing. 'But I do find sitting around tends to…well…' she turned slightly, drawing a seductive hand over her non-existent hips, '…add a little in the wrong spot.'

'Nothing that shows,' Abbie remarked cheerfully.

'Well, no…' Venetia blinked.

'Coffee?' Cas interrupted, making a sign to the waiter.

'Oh, lovely,' Venetia said, and beamed.

Abbie sighed inwardly. She would have liked to have whispered to Cas that the roses would be dying of thirst. But then he'd know she'd been watching him and, anyway, surely Venetia couldn't take another half-hour to drink coffee?

'Is there anywhere around here that's nice to go afterwards?' Venetia asked as they sipped very hot liquid from demitasse cups.

'Clubs aren't really Tilly's style,' Abbie replied cheerfully. 'But you'd probably find something along the coast.'

Cas threw her a black look. 'We hadn't planned on anything,' he asserted quickly, but Venetia pouted.

'Oh, I'd love to go on somewhere.'

Abbie stared innocently at Cas. 'You haven't drunk anything tonight. And you haven't got to be up early in the morning.'

He looked thunderous. 'I know, but—' he began, but Venetia was already throwing her arms around him.

'Cas, darling, really? Oh, I simply knew this was going to be a wonderful weekend.'

'They happen occasionally,' Abbie remarked dryly, and stood up. 'Don't bother about me. I'll call a taxi.'

'Oh, don't you want to come with us?' Venetia tried to look disappointed and failed.

'Abbie!' Cas protested, untangling himself, but Abbie pressed him down on his chair.

'You two have a wonderful night.' She smiled benignly, and did something with her hands, which Cas would, no doubt, have called fluttering, as she walked sedately from the restaurant.

Despite the old world charm of the King's Head and the undisputed excellence of the Dover sole, Abbie breathed a long sigh of relief. The receptionist called her a taxi and she scrambled into it.

It wasn't listening to Venetia all night that had been so depressing. It was the way Cas had gazed at Venetia with deep brown eyes that begged for more.

Well, he could have more.

But Abbie definitely wasn't going to be there to witness it.

CHAPTER NINE

SHE had two options.

Since she was wide awake she could either wait up—watch TV or do some work in the office—or go to bed and probably not sleep anyway. It was a quarter to eleven, so it could mean a long night. And what if they stayed out all night? What if—and Abbie's mind whirled imaginatively ahead—Cas stayed out *all* night.

Well, that wasn't impossible. In fact, it was very probable, Abbie decided as she let herself into the house and flicked on the hall light. She wondered what Cas was doing right now. Dancing with Venetia, probably. Or sitting in some dark corner in a romantic mood.

'Well, that's OK.' Abbie told herself as she went upstairs. 'They were obviously made for each other.'

In her bedroom, she caught the reflection of herself in the mirror. She quickly replaced the look of dismay on her face with a smile and tossed back her hair. For a moment she remembered how Cas had untangled the clip, his fingers making her heart do a little jiggle. And how he had said she had beautiful hair.

Abbie moved closer to the mirror and peered at her wayward curls. She'd always been desperate to unravel them into a long, silky bob. Like Venetia's. She'd lost count of the hairdressers who had tried.

In the end, she'd given up. Accepted the fact that the trait was hereditary. And she'd almost forgotten that little longing until tonight. Or, rather, until yesterday afternoon, when she'd met Venetia.

'Stop it, Abbie Scott,' she told herself sternly. 'This is obsessive behaviour.' The remedy for which was a long, sudsy soak, an indecently early night and a book.

The bath worked out pretty well. She pampered herself, submerged in bubbles for half an hour. When she climbed out, she massaged the remainder of the baby oil into her skin and strictly prohibited serious thought.

It was only when she saw her dress lying on the bed that it flooded back. Cas's tall figure and the roses. Venetia's little stories of how they'd met. And Cas's expression as he'd watched her.

Abbie hung up the dress and went to make herself a hot drink. She tried not to think of how empty the house felt. Or how she missed hearing

Cas's footfall on the stairs. Or listening to the plumbing when he used excessive water in the bathroom upstairs.

Instead, she took her drink upstairs, found a book and lay in bed, reflecting that ultimately she was going back to America. Thinking about Cas and who he was out with and what they were doing was a pointless exercise.

Neither sleep nor interest in what she was reading materialised. In the end, she simply lay there and gazed out at a crescent moon under which—somewhere—Cas and Venetia would be…together.

Abbie knew she was dreaming, because she was looking up into eyes that she would have recognised anywhere. They were gazing down on her—and not Venetia. Who, thankfully, hadn't made an appearance *anywhere* in the dream.

They were deliriously beautiful brown eyes with little black flecks swirling around in their centres and desire written in them, as Cas's mouth came down slowly, covering her lips with passion that had her heart pounding so wildly she couldn't breathe.

Of course, the reality was that if she couldn't breathe, she couldn't kiss back either. But this was a dream and that's how he'd made her feel when he'd kissed her for real. Like anything could happen. His image was so clear she could have reached out to touch him. Thread her fingers through the dark, glossy hair which—in her dream—hadn't been cut and still hung rebelliously around his collar. And with just one small adjustment to his hand around her waist, she could believe that he really was kissing her as that hand travelled up and over the low back of her green dress with seductive little movements that had her wanting more. Much more.

So she closed her eyes, yielding her body…

And woke.

The bedside light was on and she was hot and disorientated. What was it that had woken her? She hauled herself crossly out of bed, weaved into the middle of the room and frowned at her bag on the dressing-table.

'Mobile,' she grumbled, and rummaged it out.

'Yes?'

There was a long pause and a few odd noises. Abbie wondered if it was a hoax call. She could forgive someone for a wrong number, but not a heavy breather at this time of night. Especially since she had been in the process of dreaming an irreplaceable dream.

'Yes? Who is it?' she demanded again.

'Dr Scott?' a tiny voice said.

'Charlie?'

'Y-yes.'

'What's wrong?' Abbie came quickly awake. 'It's...' She peered at her watch. 'Almost three o'clock in the morning.'

'I know. I'm really sorry. But I...I'm not at Nanna's, Dr Scott. You were the only one I could think of to call. And I had your mobile number. I know it's the middle of the night but—'

'Where are you, Charlie?'

'In Exeter,' Charlie replied tearfully.

'*Exeter?*' Abbie gasped. 'What are you doing there?'

'Some friends brought me. Or at least I thought they were friends before they dumped me. I haven't got any money to come home, Dr Scott.'

'Tell me exactly where you are and I'll pick you up.' Abbie dragged her notebook from her bag. Charlie's voice was faint and she only managed to take a few details before the reception faded altogether.

It would take an hour or so, if she was lucky, to find Charlie. But why was Charlie miles away from home at this time of night? Abbie threw on jeans and as an afterthought collected her case from the surgery.

She was about to leave when she saw a chink of light under the lounge door. Had she left it on? She couldn't remember going in there. But perhaps she had.

Pushing the door open, she saw Cas sprawled on the sofa. His legs were spread out in front of him and his head had fallen onto his chest. His jacket was thrown casually over the arm of the sofa. He must have come home whilst she'd been asleep.

What had happened to Venetia? she wondered as she closed the door slowly. Abbie was almost out of the front door when a voice boomed behind her.

'Bit late to go out, isn't it?'

She turned to find Cas standing there. Both hands were screwed down in his pockets and his shirt looked rumpled. A dark shadow crept over his chin and his tone was disgruntled.

'I didn't want to wake you—' she began, but he cut her short.

'Thanks. Very thoughtful.'

'Cas, I haven't time to stop—'

'Obviously not,' he muttered.

'I just had a call from Charlie,' she explained hurriedly. 'She's in Exeter, of all places, without any money. She said her friends dumped her there.'

He cursed under his breath and came towards her. 'Is she all right?'

'I don't know. But I managed to get an idea of where she is—'

'An *idea*?' he repeated, frowning as he stood there.

'She said she was in a café and gave me some, well…rather vague directions.'

He lifted his eyes to the ceiling. 'Wonderful. A café! At this time of night. And you thought you'd sneak off on your own?'

'Well…you don't have to come with me.' She shrugged, wishing that she hadn't gone into the lounge and disturbed him.

'Of course I don't. I'll just sit here and twiddle my thumbs, not worrying, shall I?' He dragged his hands raggedly over his face. 'What about the police? Shouldn't we call them first?'

'I'd rather not—yet. Charlie phoned here, Cas. Which means—'

'Which means she's been up to something and doesn't want anyone to find out,' he sighed, rolling down his shirtsleeves. 'Wait a moment and I'll get my jacket.'

Five minutes later, they were sitting in the four-wheel-drive and Cas was flicking on the headlights.

'What brought you home early anyway?' Abbie asked.

He gave a dark little smile and changed gear. 'I'm out of practice,' he told her shortly, 'in the art of partying.'

'Oh.'

'Exactly.'

'You've probably been living in the sticks for too long,' she suggested brightly.

'Yes,' he agreed. 'Venetia said the same.'

Which is exactly what I deserve for asking, Abbie thought.

Charlie had given Abbie the name of a street, so they asked at a petrol station on the outskirts of Exeter and were given directions.

'No café,' Cas said as he slowed down, frowning out at the darkened houses. 'It's a residential area.'

'I must have the wrong name. There was so much interference on the line. Let's try down there.' The road swerved off to the right but it was clear there was nothing at the end of it, just more residential houses.

'Great,' Abbie sighed as they turned into the main road again and headed for the town centre. 'Now what?'

'You don't have her mobile number by any chance?' Cas asked, throwing her a hopeful glance.

'No. I didn't have time to ask. Look, we could get directions in there.' Abbie pointed to a petrol station. 'There might be someone around.'

There wasn't. It was shut and the kiosk deserted. 'Not a soul in sight,' Cas muttered. 'I still think we should go to the police.'

'What about these people?' Abbie suggested, and nodded towards a couple walking along the road. 'Let's try one last time.'

Cas drove toward the young man and woman and Abbie stuck her head out of the window. When she'd explained what they were looking for, the young man shook his head.

'Can't think of an all night café,' the man said.

'There's the transport caf,' his girlfriend suggested. 'There's one down the road.'

They gave Abbie directions and she thanked them. Cas muttered under his breath about a wild-goose chase. But they found the place and its lights were on.

The café smelt pleasantly of breakfast, but the woman behind the counter frowned as they approached.

'I'm looking for a friend,' Abbie explained quickly, noting two burly truck-drivers glance up. 'A young girl, with her hair in braids—'

'Who are you?' the woman interrupted. 'And who's he?'

'We're doctors,' Abbie said, realising the woman was staring at them suspiciously. 'And our friend's name is Charlotte—Charlie for short.'

'Wait a moment.' The woman disappeared behind the counter. 'You'd better follow me.'

They trailed through the kitchen, where a man was cooking at a range, then into a back room. Here, a TV was on as they entered and Charlie sprang up from a chair in front of it.

'Dr Scott—Dr Darke!'

The woman smiled as Charlie hurtled into Abbie's arms. 'Would you like some tea?' she asked, and Abbie nodded over Charlie's shoulder.

'Yes, we'd love some, thank you.'

'I'm so sorry,' Charlie apologised tearfully. 'I didn't know what to do. And I didn't want to frighten Nanna.'

Cas went over to the TV and turned it off. He pulled out one of the chairs at the table and sat down. 'What happened, Charlie?'

'It was awful. Some people I know phoned Nanna's on Friday afternoon. They said there was a party somewhere down this way and would I like to go.'

'What did your grandmother have to say about that?' Cas asked as Charlie sat down at the table.

'Well, she wasn't there,' Charlie admitted, going red. 'She'd gone out to supper with a friend in Tilly.'

'So you went without speaking to her about it?'

'I left her a message, saying I had decided to go away for the weekend and that I'd ring her today.'

'Don't you know that your grandmother would be very worried about you, Charlie?' Cas said quietly.

Charlie dropped her head and wept.

'Charlie, are you all right?' Abbie asked. 'You're not hurt?'

Charlie shook her head and the door swung open. The owner of the café came in with three mugs of tea and placed them on the table. She arched an eyebrow at Charlie. 'I told her she's a very lucky girl.' The woman smiled at Cas and Abbie. 'I'm Joan Brown, by the way. Me and my husband run the café.'

'It was good of you to take care of Charlie,' Abbie said, and Joan shrugged.

'Well, I expect she'll tell you all about it in her own good time. But my advice to this young lady is to get herself some new friends. The lot she was with took all her money and then disappeared.'

'I'm sorry I've caused you all so much trouble,' Charlie said, peering at them with puffy eyes.

'Did you phone your grandmother?' Cas asked.

Charlie nodded. 'This afternoon.'

'What did you tell her?'

'She thinks I'm in London at my dad's house.'

'Where have you been since Friday night?'

Charlie shrugged. 'We went to this party on Friday night and I slept on the floor. Then we hung about in the town after I'd phoned Nanna. Then we went on to this other house, but…well…it wasn't my scene,' she added, not looking at them. 'So I asked someone to drive me to the station. We got in his van, but we never got to the station. He made me give him what money I had and told me to get out.'

'Lucky one of the blokes saw her wandering round the car park,' Joan sighed. 'She was in a right old state. He brought her in and my husband said we should phone the police, but she didn't want that and said she'd phone you instead.'

They all sat in silence for a while. Then Cas finished his tea and thanked Joan and her husband for what they'd done for Charlie. They left the little café as dawn broke and Charlie curled up in the back and fell asleep.

They didn't talk much on the way home. Cas drove grimly through the darkness and Abbie's tired thoughts veered from Charlie's dangerous exploits to the hallucinatory vision of red roses. Had Venetia liked them? But she was too weary, even, to be jealous.

Fibber, she told herself as she forced her eyes to stay open. You're just pretending you're not.

'You won't tell Nanna, will you?'

Abbie thought that Charlie, showered and fed and after five hours of sleep, looked chastened.

'I won't. Because I don't want to worry her either,' Abbie admitted as they sat in the garden and ate lunch. 'But I'm concerned about you, Charlie. I know there's more going on in your life than you want to talk about.'

Charlie was silent and Abbie looked at her. 'You're worried about your grandmother and that shows you care. But it's you I'm concerned about. One day you won't be so lucky.'

'I know I was lucky. I had you to help me—'

'I don't mean that,' Abbie said, and raised an eyebrow. 'I mean that, if you're not careful you're going to get into stuff that will be more difficult to stop taking.'

'How do you know about that?' Charlie asked, going red again.

'I work with people in a rehab clinic. And I know what temptations there are for you. But, Charlie, you have a good brain and a sweet nature. You've so much potential. Don't waste it.'

Charlie looked down at her hands and sat quietly. 'I'm not into smoking in a big way,' she murmured. 'I've only done it a few times and I don't even really like it.'

'Then don't do it. Make new friends and find something you love to do. You'll get enough excitement from having a focus in life.'

'I'm not going to hang out with those guys any more,' Charlie said sincerely. 'My stepmother never liked them. I think I did it more to annoy her.'

'It's not a perfect world, Charlie. Parents come in all shapes and sizes.'

'I know. I think I was jealous of Dad. I just didn't want him to fall in love with anyone else after Mum died.'

Abbie nodded slowly. 'The little green devil isn't so little, is he?'

Charlie looked up. 'Your mother died when you were young, Nanna said. She told me about how you used to come and visit.'

Abbie nodded slowly. 'Your grandparents were very kind to me. Like you, I missed my mum a lot.' Abbie smiled. 'What do you plan on doing when you go home from your grandmother's?'

'I don't know.'

'You're very good with the patients. Do you enjoy this kind of work?'

Charlie nodded. 'I love it here.'

'Well, something within a medical environment might suit you. You've your IT qualifications and Caspar and I will be able to give you a reference.'

'Would you? I hadn't thought about that.'

Abbie saw Cas strolling across the lawn and nodded. 'We'll talk about it later on. But now I'd better drive you home.'

Charlie sprang to her feet and beamed a smile at Cas. 'I'll just get my bag.'

'Recovered, I see,' he said dryly as Charlie disappeared. 'Did you grab some sleep this morning?'

Abbie nodded. 'And you?'

'The last thing I remember was you installing Charlie in one of the spare rooms before my head hit the pillow.'

'We had a little talk, Charlie and I,' Abbie explained. 'I suggested a job in the health sector—and I've volunteered references.'

'Have you, now?' He sank down onto the chair beside her. 'What makes you think she'll go for it?'

'Instinct?'

One dark eyebrow crooked. 'I hope you'll not be disappointed.' He stretched his arms, bringing the palm of his hand through his hair and down his neck to flop back on the arm of the chair. They were both wearing shorts and T-shirts and Abbie was wondering if he had rung Greg Wise to cover surgery. Obviously he had, she decided, or he would have dressed in something more formal.

'Any plans for today?' he asked, almost reading her thoughts.

She shook her head. 'Nothing special.'

'If you've nothing in mind, after Charlie's landed, perhaps we cou—' Cas stared at the house and Abbie followed his gaze as Charlie appeared on the lawn. Beside her was Venetia.

'Now what?' Cas groaned. 'I thought she was driving back this morning.'

'Hi,' Venetia called. 'I'm so glad I found you in.'

'Time for me to take Charlie home,' Abbie said, and got up as Cas threw her a frown.

'Thank goodness,' Venetia sighed as she sank down into Abbie's chair. 'I've been looking for a garage but they all seem to be closed.'

'It's Sunday.' Cas shrugged. 'Why do you want a garage?'

'There's a noise coming from under the bonnet,' Venetia trilled, tossing back her blonde hair and arranging the folds of her dress. 'I wondered if you'd take a look at it for me.'

Abbie had the satisfaction of seeing Cas's face fall before she left. But Charlie soon brought her back to earth. 'She's very attractive, isn't she?' Charlie whispered as she walked beside Abbie to the house.

'Yes, very.'

'But not Dr Darke's sort.'

'What makes you say that?'

'Nothing.' Charlie went pink. 'I just don't think he'd have much in common with her, really. Not like you.'

It was Abbie's turn to blush. She muttered something about never judging books by their covers, but it didn't seem to wash with Charlie.

Who insisted on talking about Cas all the way back to her grandmother's.

It was the middle of July when Abbie next visited the Dunnings. Five weeks after her birth, little Joanne had turned the Dunning household upside down.

'She's always hungry,' Susan complained. 'It's as though I haven't got enough to satisfy her.'

'She's been weighed at the clinic?' Abbie asked, thinking how bonny the baby looked curled contentedly in her mother's arms.

Susan nodded. 'But she never seems to sleep.'

'I think she should be fed and then left to cry,' Marjorie Ellis interrupted as she came into the lounge. 'It's not good to keep picking them up all the time.'

'I don't like to hear her cry,' Susan responded sharply. 'And it's different now. People feed on demand.'

'Well, I don't know much about babies,' Marjorie insisted, pushing back her tight grey perm, 'but I know enough to believe that a feed should last her longer than an hour or so.'

'She might not have had enough,' Susan protested.

'Nonsense,' snapped Marjorie.

'Not at it again, is she?' Bob said as he came into the room and sat down to pull off his wellingtons.

Susan sighed and rolled her eyes.

'Never had any of our lot waking up every five minutes in the night,' Bob complained loudly. 'This one's like a foghorn.'

'I told Susan just to leave her,' Marjorie began, but Susan stood up, clutching the baby against her.

'Leave us alone, all of you,' she yelped, which made Joanne give out a shriek of protest. As the baby continued to scream, Susan burst into tears.

'I'd like to check her.' Abbie just managed to make herself heard above Joanne's wails. 'Perhaps in your room?'

Susan nodded and Marjorie scuttled out to the kitchen.

Bob stood up. 'Women!' he groaned. 'I want my Josie home.'

'How is she?' Abbie asked as she, too, stood up.

'Not so good, really. A bit depressed.'

As Abbie followed Susan up to her room, she made a mental note to call on Josie. Not that it seemed a good idea for her to return home whilst the baby was so young. Susan had returned to her old moody self and would probably remain the same until she was more confident with Joanne.

Abbie found Susan sitting on the bed, changing Joanne's nappy. As she raised her from the baby mattress, the baby gurgled happily.

'She already has good control over her head,' Abbie said, sitting on the end of the bed. 'She's coming along well.'

'Her neck muscles are really strong,' Susan sniffed. 'And so are her lungs.'

Abbie smiled. 'Does she really wake you a lot in the nights?'

Susan shrugged. 'I don't mind.'

'Are you getting any sleep?'

Susan nodded, but Abbie could see the hollows around her eyes.

'Are you afraid she'll wake everyone?'

'You heard Marjorie and Dad. They're light sleepers. If Mum was here…' Susan stopped and bit her lip. 'I miss her a lot. I wish she was home.'

'It might be some time before she's well again,' Abbie said quietly.

Susan looked up. 'How long?'

'I don't know,' Abbie admitted. 'Maybe weeks or even months.'

'But it's awful here,' Susan said quickly. 'Aunt Marjorie is driving me mad.'

'Your mum will need specialised help, Sue,' Abbie continued gently. 'She wouldn't be able to help with the baby, not even by holding her— not with her arm the way it is.'

Susan hugged Joanne against her. 'I don't think Dad or Marjorie even like the baby. Mum would adore her.'

'Have you been in to visit her yet?' Abbie asked curiously.

'She told Dad she didn't want me to visit whilst Joanne is so young. In case there's an infection in the hospital. Mum's like that. She's so caring.'

'Have you thought about going to stay with one of your sisters?' Abbie suggested. 'For a holiday?'

'No,' Susan said firmly. 'There's only Rachel and Sarah living in England. The other two emigrated. Rachel has a partner who doesn't want children. I can hardly expect him to like mine if he doesn't want one of his own. And Sarah only has a bedsit in Plymouth.'

It seemed, as usual, that Susan's problems were insurmountable, and finally Abbie left. Perhaps, Abbie reflected, it would cheer her up if Cas called. So the following day, Thursday, she decided to speak to him about the Dunnings.

But when she came downstairs to breakfast, Cas was already in the office. She paused, watching his dark head bent over the papers that Charlie had filed the day before. His brow was furrowed and he seemed deep in thought.

Abbie went into the kitchen without disturbing him. There would be time to mention Susan later. She realised that since Venetia had visited, he had spent more and more time in the field next door.

The building had a roof on now and Abbie had watched its slow but relentless progress. There was interest, too, in the house. The agent had said that he hoped to have confirmation of a buyer. Abbie didn't want to think about it. Instead, in her spare time, she buried the smaller articles in newspaper, packed them in boxes and stacked them out of sight.

Charlie had settled back into her routine and Eve, fortunately, had never questioned Charlie's absence that weekend.

Abbie ate a swift breakfast and decided to talk to Cas about Susan before surgery. But as she approached the office she could hear Cas on the phone. When she walked in, Cas's face was grim and he signalled her to sit down.

'You'll let us know if you hear anything?' he asked. When he replaced the phone, he spoke curtly. 'Susan Dunning has gone missing—again. Only this time she's got the baby with her.'

CHAPTER TEN

'YOU saw her?' Cas said after Abbie had finished explaining that she'd visited Susan yesterday. 'Did she say anything—give you any clue as to why she might disappear?'

Abbie paused. 'Well, she's not getting on with Marjorie. And she misses Josie. But I didn't think she'd go so far as to leave home.'

'She must have gone in the night,' Cas said, standing and clipping his mobile phone to his belt. 'Bob said her bed hadn't been slept in.'

'Has he called the police?' Abbie asked anxiously.

'Yes, but a twenty-nine-year-old woman staying out all night doesn't constitute an emergency.'

'But she has the baby.'

'Marjorie said they'd quarrelled over Joanne late last night.' Cas shrugged. 'The pushchair's gone, so Sue must have left the farm on foot.'

'What about clothes—possessions—stuff for the baby?'

Cas picked up his case and opened the office door. 'Nothing's been taken apparently. I'm going to have a scout round. Look down at the beach and on the cliffs. Then I'll come back here and collect you.'

'I've surgery until midday.' Abbie added hopefully, 'Maybe she'll even turn up by that time.'

Cas didn't look convinced. 'Is Charlie in today?'

'No, she's having a morning off.'

'Can you cope here?'

She nodded. 'I'm fine. Cas...'

He turned and raised an eyebrow, his dark eyes locking with hers.

'Before...when you found Sue...do you really think she would have done something to harm herself?'

He shrugged his broad shoulders and sighed. 'It's anyone's guess. But I don't think we can take this lightly. I'm going to speak to the police first. Hammer home that this might not just be a family fight—which is what they'll think, no doubt.'

Abbie watched him go and wondered where Susan could have got to. If she had left the farm during the night, she would have been on foot. Had she taken the pushchair? If only she had been able to reassure Susan about Josie. Maybe that would have prevented her from leaving.

On the other hand, anything less than the truth about Josie's condition would have only caused repercussions later.

The morning dragged by. Her mind kept going to Susan and little Joanne. Where could they be? If Susan was depressed she might not be able to look after the baby properly. And yet Abbie hadn't felt that she was seriously depressed. Just missing Josie and feeling strung out with Marjorie's interference.

The open surgery resulted in a few summer colds and coughs and one of the workmen from next door pulled a muscle in his back. She told him to rest and advised a light painkiller, and by eleven-thirty the little waiting room was empty.

Cas returned just after twelve but the news was grim. Susan hadn't been seen by anyone. 'The police are looking along the beach,' Cas told her. 'I've done a search along the cliffs where I last found her. I'm going to change, then maybe we should have look around Tilly.'

Abbie nodded. 'Have we any visits?'

'No, thank God. Meet you outside in ten minutes.'

Abbie changed into cotton trousers and a loose shirt and sneakers. Wherever they went, she might be climbing over or into things. And her mind went into overdrive at the possibilities.

Cas must have been thinking the same, she realised, because he, too, had exchanged his smart linen trousers for jeans and a cool blue T-shirt.

'Have you any idea where she might have gone?' Cas asked as he reversed the vehicle out of the drive.

'No...' Abbie hesitated. 'Unless she went to her old flat.'

'The one she was evicted from?'

Abbie nodded. 'Josie said it was by the market. Over the auction rooms.'

'OK. We'll try there first.'

The flat was accessed by a winding spiral staircase at the back of the auction rooms. Though the place was in need of a lick of paint, Abbie noticed that there were window-boxes and people had made an effort to brighten up the rear yards with garden furniture and potted shrubs.

'Poor Sue,' Abbie sighed as they climbed to the top of the staircase. 'It's cosy here. No wonder she was upset at leaving.'

The flat was occupied by new tenants and Cas explained the purpose of their visit.

'She left some things here,' the man said, showing them through into the flat. 'We've put them in a box. You can have them if you like.'

Cas glanced at Abbie and then back at the young man. 'I'll take them to her father.'

'If she does come back here,' Abbie said to the girl, 'could you let us know? Here's my card with my mobile number.'

The girl nodded, then paused. 'The guy—Ralf his name was, I think—called too. He came to collect an old TV, he said. But he kept asking questions about the girl you're looking for. Where she was and what had happened to her.'

'How long ago was this?' Cas asked.

'Early this year, just after we moved in.'

Cas took the box and they left, but Abbie stopped him as he opened the back door of the vehicle.

'Should we look inside?' she suggested. 'There might be something to help us.'

Cas nodded and heaved the box into the back seat. They sat on either side of it and began to look through Susan's meagre possessions—photos, ornaments, cutlery and little pieces of china.

'This must be Ralf,' Abbie said, and passed Cas a photo of Susan in happier times, smiling up at a tall, blond, bearded man.

'He looks harmless and happy enough.' Cas shrugged. 'I wonder what went wrong.'

'The baby, apparently,' Abbie said softly. 'He left Sue when she was pregnant.'

'I wonder if there's more to it than Susan said,' Cas murmured as he tucked the photo back into the box, then frowned at the small badge Abbie was holding. 'What's that?'

'A school badge. I had one just like it. Susan must have kept hers. Though I'm surprised. She didn't like school much.'

'What was she like as a kid?' Cas asked curiously. 'A good mixer, or a loner?'

'A bit of an outsider,' Abbie said reflectively. 'Unlike her older sisters.'

Cas nodded, exhaling slowly. 'Well, I'm stumped.'

'Me, too.' Abbie rubbed her finger pensively over the little badge. Suddenly she looked up. 'Cas, perhaps she's gone to the school.'

'Why should she go there?'

Abbie shook her head slowly. 'I don't know. A walk down memory lane perhaps? It's worth a try.'

Ten minutes later Cas parked outside the old Victorian red-brick school and squinted across the deserted playground. 'Closed for the summer holidays,' he murmured. 'I wonder if the caretaker's on duty?'

'Let's have a look round the back,' Cas suggested.

But once they arrived at the back of the building everywhere appeared secure. Abbie pointed to an L-shaped annexe. 'That was our classroom.'

'Is there a rear entrance?'

'Yes, just around there.'

They walked slowly around the classroom and Abbie was beginning to feel they had wasted their time when she heard a noise.

'Did you hear that?' She looked at Cas and he nodded.

'It sounded like a baby's cries.'

He jerked his head to the door that appeared to be locked. But when he turned the handle the door squeaked open. The noise came clearly this time and Abbie found herself running alongside him.

'You try the rooms on that side,' Cas called. 'I'll go along here.'

Abbie went to the first classroom but it was locked, then to the next but with no luck. Cas did the same on the other side and when he got to the third door he gestured to her to follow him. 'The lock's been forced,' he told her as he pushed open the door. 'Look. And someone's tried to start a fire in a waste-paper basket. It must be some bored local kids.'

'Lucky it didn't catch,' Abbie sighed, looking around. 'I dread to think what would have happened if it had.'

Just then the sounds came again and they rushed back into the corridor. 'It's the caretaker's cupboard,' Abbie cried. 'That's Sue's voice!'

When they came to the cupboard, Abbie's heart sank. It was a solid wooden door and Sue's cries and the baby's were coming from behind it. Cas tried it several times, then shouldered it before shaking his head. 'Susan, it's me, Caspar. And Abbie's with me.'

Susan was sobbing and Abbie had to shout to make herself heard. 'We're going to get you out, Sue. Be patient a few moments more.'

'I'm going to get some tools,' Cas told her. 'I'll be as quick as I can.'

Abbie nodded and, alone with Sue, she spoke reassuringly, but Sue was too distraught to reply properly, though Abbie could just gather that some boisterous lads had shoved Sue into the cupboard. When Cas returned, he broke open the lock with the tools from his vehicle and light flooded the small, dark room. Amidst shelves of polish, buckets, mops and brooms were Sue and the baby. She burst into tears and Abbie bent down and put her arms around her.

'You're going to be fine,' she whispered.

Then they helped her to her feet and slowly made their way along the corridor, into the warmth and brightness of the summer's day.

Abbie laid Joanne in her pushchair, tucked the cotton sheet under her tiny chin and glanced at Susan who was buttoning up her dress. She looked pale and tired, but she had fed Joanne and changed her and had eventually composed herself.

Abbie wondered if, whilst she and Susan had been sitting in the surgery, Cas had managed to speak to Bob and the police. Had Susan wanted to go straight home, they could have phoned from the farm, but Susan had expressed no wish to return. And it had been Cas's suggestion that perhaps it would be better for Susan to remain for a few hours at Tilly House. He had left them alone, hoping that whilst little Joanne slept, Susan would feel like talking.

As luck would have it, Joanne's eyelids fluttered to a close and Susan sat back in the big leather chair and sighed. 'If only she'd do that more often.'

'She fed so well because she was hungry,' Abbie said quietly.

'So Aunt Marjorie has got a point?' Susan murmured, and glanced up. 'She says I'm always giving in to Joanne's demands. But if I don't, she cries and—'

'It's a vicious circle.' Abbie nodded. 'And it's very easy to talk about someone else's baby.'

'That's what I think,' Susan said sharply, her old aggressiveness surfacing. Then she shook her head defeatedly. 'I suppose all this trouble will give Aunt Marjorie something else to complain about.'

'What happened, Sue?' Abbie asked gently.

Sue's chin wobbled but she managed to re-cover herself. 'We had a blazing row last night, about Joanne. I said some awful things to Aunt Marjorie about poking her nose in. And she said I was just like Mum, stubborn and wilful, and that I'd come to a bad end, just like Mum. So I told her what I thought of her. That she's a dried-up old spinster who doesn't know what life is all about.'

'And that was when you left?'

Susan eyes widened in surprise. 'No, I just went to my room and prayed Joanne wouldn't wake up and start crying. It seems every time she does, my aunt tries to tell me what I'm doing wrong. And I'd just about had enough.'

'But your father said your bed hadn't been slept in.'

'No, I didn't go to bed. Joanne woke and I fed her. Or at least I tried to. But she sensed I was upset, I think. So I put her in her pushchair and rocked her—the only way to keep her quiet. And I wasn't going to let Aunt Marjorie say I told you so one more time!' Susan lifted her chin determinedly. 'I was sitting in the chair, rocking the pram all night on and off. Then when it got light, I thought, I might as well push her out in the fresh air. Then I wouldn't be worried about waking anyone. I decided to take the little path across Dad's fallow field and we finally ended up in Tilly. It was such a beautiful day.'

'But why did you go to the school?'

Susan sighed softly. 'I just found myself walking past it and thinking how Joanne would probably go there. Odd, isn't it? History repeating itself. Then I saw an outside door ajar and I went in.' Susan sniffed and held back the tears.

'So you just walked into school…through an open door?' Abbie said slowly. 'Didn't you think it was unusual to find a door unlocked?'

Susan shrugged. 'Not really. Mr Whiffen, our old caretaker, used to unlock the doors when he was cleaning. Remember? Anyway, I didn't think anyone would mind me and Joanne having a quick look around. So I pushed the pushchair along the corridor and saw the cupboard open.

Then all of a sudden someone came up behind me and bundled me and Joanne in the cupboard and locked it.'

'It was a shock to find you there, Sue,' Abbie conceded. 'Did you see who it was that pushed you inside?'

'Not really. I just had the impression it was some young kids. I heard them running down the corridor and it all went quiet. There's only that little window up high in the cupboard and I couldn't see anything. I just hoped the caretaker would find us. But as time went on I got more and more scared.'

Not wanting to alarm Susan more, Abbie didn't mention they had found evidence that someone had tried to start a fire in the corridor. And when Cas came back into the room, it was with good news.

'I spoke to the police and your father, Susan. I told him that we'd return you home in a little while. The police are going to the school and, no doubt, will want to have a word with you later.'

Susan nodded slowly. 'Was Dad angry?'

'No, just relieved to know that you and Joanne are OK.' Cas heaved in a breath and patted the hard, flat wall of his abdomen. 'I've stuck some bacon under the grill,' he grinned, jerking an eyebrow. 'Any offers?'

Cas cooked them all a snack and listened to Susan's story, his gaze occasionally flicking to Abbie. She watched him put Susan at ease and turn out a pretty good meal and wonderful coffee, all whilst appearing to carefully digest the problems of the Dunning family.

He didn't hide his amusement when Susan related what she had said to Marjorie. And the quarrel's bite seemed to lose its sting as a result. He told her that she should take the situation more lightly. That Marjorie wouldn't be around for ever. And that Josie would finally come home.

'And,' he continued as he devoured the last lavishly buttered slice of toast, 'we've got some of your things in a box. The people at the flat gave them to us.'

Susan looked surprised. 'You went there?'

Abbie nodded. 'To look for you.'

'Did you know Ralf went back there?' Cas said, swallowing and gulping coffee.

'No. When?'

'Not long after they moved in. He asked after you.'

'Did he?' Susan went pink. 'Did they say any more about him?'

Abbie met Cas's eyes and this time she knew what he was going to say. He rubbed a finger thoughtfully around the edge of his mug. 'Would I be right in guessing he doesn't know about the baby?'

It was a long shot. But Abbie saw the change in Susan's expression. And she wasn't surprised when tears plopped over her lids.

'No.'

'Don't you think he should?' Cas said quietly.

'It wouldn't make any difference.' She sniffed and looked up. 'How did you know?'

'The girl said he asked after you—not a mention of the baby. If he asked all those questions, the baby would have figured in it somewhere. Unless he was a fairly hard-hearted soul. And he didn't look it.'

'You saw him?' Susan gulped.

'No,' Cas said softly. 'Just a photo. And he looked a pretty normal guy.'

Sue nodded and the tears fell again. 'He was. It was me. I just couldn't accept he loved me. I think I drove him away.'

'Well, he has a daughter, a beautiful little girl. Who, one day, will want to know who her father is.' Cas glanced at Abbie and the message in his eyes was clear.

'Do you know where Ralf is?' Abbie asked Susan.

She shook her head quickly. 'He has a sister, though.'

Though no more was said whilst they cleared the dishes, Abbie felt that Susan's attitude had changed. Whether it was because of her experience this morning at the school or Cas's intuitive guess, she didn't know. Maybe, she decided hopefully, a mixture of both.

'Thanks, Abbie,' she said before Cas took her home.

'Good luck, Sue.' Abbie hugged her and helped her into the vehicle with the baby. She watched the vehicle disappear down the track, went back inside and wondered what sort of reception Sue would receive when she got home.

If the experiences and the feedback from today did anything for Susan, it might strengthen her resolve to face certain issues. On the other hand, she might just fall back into her old ways, hold onto the crutch of conflict with her family and sadly forget the relationship she'd begun with Joanne's father.

Surgery was crammed the following morning. Amongst them was Reggie Donaldson, the auctioneer, who had caught flu. A summer bug had felled his wife and, it seemed, almost half of Tilly.

'I feel rough,' Reggie complained as he sat in the chair, sweating and wheezing. 'My legs don't feel my own.'

'You're still on them,' Abbie pointed out, taking his temperature which was certainly up. 'You say your wife's in bed.'

'Yes.' He nodded. 'At least I haven't got a sore throat.'

'How is the yoga going?'

'I'll let you know in a week's time after my next hospital appointment,' he told her cautiously.

'Would you like me to call in later and see your wife?' Abbie asked as she sat down, but Reggie shook his head.

'She'd have to be drawing her last breath to see a doctor,' he said, managing a smile. 'Now, what are you going to give me to clear this lot up?'

'A little advice,' Abbie said dryly. 'Put your feet up and rest, take paracetamol and drink lots of fluid.'

'But I've got a big auction coming up after the weekend,' Reggie protested. 'I need to be firing on all cylinders for Monday.'

'I can't see why you shouldn't be.' Abbie shrugged. 'As long as you don't get stressed and undo all the good work your yoga exercises have done.'

'You sound like my other half,' Reggie grunted, and stood up.

'Let me know how the hospital appointment goes,' Abbie said as he was about to leave. He nodded. 'And keep up with your yoga.'

A remark that caused Reggie to lift his eyes as he disappeared out of the door.

Reggie wasn't the first to complain of the bug, and people turned up with sore throats and achy legs which caused Cas to be busy for most of the day.

The casualties continued into the evening and through to the following day. Greg Wise went down with it and Tilly House took the burden of calls for the two villages.

On Sunday morning the flow seemed to have eased. There were two early calls, but neither for the bug. Both were hospital referrals.

'One appendix,' Abbie told Cas when she returned. 'One early labour. But no flu bugs, thank God.' She found him in the office, his head hidden in the most recent NHS missives.

He looked up and stretched like a lazy cat. 'Bad night?'

She nodded. 'One of Greg's patients at three-thirty. An elderly lady with an angina attack.'

'How was she?'

Abbie shrugged and sank wearily down beside him. 'Frightened. She was out of her medication.'

He rolled his eyes. 'Had she seen Greg lately?'

'No. She's forgetful and a bit confused. I gave her glyceryl trinitrate and went over what she had to do with the spray. But I'll have to have a word in someone's ear. She needs assessment. Somehow she's escaped the net.'

Cas nodded. 'OK. As soon as Greg is over the flu, I'll let him know.' He leaned forward, his tanned arms resting easily on the desk. His eyes were dark-ringed and he looked perversely attractive in such a vulnerable state. She wished that she could sit here and look into his eyes for hours. But she needed to sleep. Her eyelids grew heavy and she stifled a yawn.

'You go and crash,' he told her. 'I'll take the calls.'

'Are you sure?'

He grinned. 'I slept for six hours. You didn't.'

She gulped back another yawn, stretched and let out a long, exhausted breath as she stood up. 'Any news from the Dunnings?'

'No,' he murmured. 'Why?'

'I just wondered. About Ralf and Susan. I thought something might come of what you said.'

He smiled regretfully. 'I'm no matchmaker. Maybe I handled it clumsily.'

'No,' she said softly. 'You didn't.'

His gaze was thoughtful. 'Heaven knows, I'm not qualified to preach on parenthood. I've put all my energy into a career and thought about little else. But for want of a bit encouragement Susan and Ralf might stand half a chance. And little Joanne might be in with a reasonable chance of two parents.'

Abbie wondered where Venetia fitted into the career part. She felt that little twang of jealousy at her ribs and tried not to conjure up the vision of Cas staring into Venetia's lovely face. And failed.

'What about the police?' she asked quickly. 'Did they find out who broke into the school?'

'No. But they did tell me the caretaker lost his car keys a few weeks ago. The cupboard key was amongst them, with a label, of all things, attached. I suppose it was a gift from heaven for the lads who found them.'

She nodded and turned. Leaning against the chair, she glanced at her watch. 'If I sleep now, we won't have anything to eat later. I was going to call at the all-day stores and forgot.'

'I'll go for beans or eggs if we're short of stuff,' he told her accommodatingly.

'I don't think we even have those.'

'Leave it to me,' he said, and grinned. 'I'll throw something together.'

'I doubt it.' She laughed. 'But I won't argue.'

'Which will be a first,' he said, and met her eyes with a teasing glimmer.

Abbie woke to a candyfloss sky, an evening chorus of blackbirds and the delicious aroma of something cooking outside. Something, she thought as she slid her legs out of bed, that hadn't been hidden in the cupboard or freezer before she'd slept.

From her window she could see the hedge and the field and a square inch or two of the back garden. Wrapped in her towelling robe, she chanced a stretch out of the window, but nearly overbalanced and ducked back in.

The smell had her stomach rumbling so she showered quickly, slid on the briefest of underwear—lacy bra and panties—and discovered a denim shift and clogs that felt cool and comfortable. She brushed out her damp hair, persuading it into a reasonable bob, then waited for it to spring back into a cap of bouncing auburn curls.

If it hadn't been for the fact she was so hungry, she would have tried again, but the aroma was far too potent and she followed her nose to the garden.

Abbie wondered if she was dreaming. A little necklace of sparkling lights was wound in the trees and glimmered and glistened amongst their leaves. Candles on sticks and in pots shone like early glow-worms. A blanket on the ground was spread with cushions and the wrought-iron table bore plates and the food. All of which seemed to be in the process of being cooked on the barbecue.

Cas, wearing khaki shorts, a tropical shirt and an irresistible pummelled straw hat, was bending down on his haunches. She watched him for a few moments, her eyes going over his long, muscled back under the shirt, his outstretched arms and strong brown fingers which seemed to be coaxing life from an ancient radio.

'Want any help?' she asked, and he turned sharply, then grinned like a guilty schoolboy.

'I'd planned to have it all done before you came down,' he told her, and finally found audible music amongst the static. It wasn't exactly blues or jazz, somewhere in between, but it seemed oddly in keeping with the evening.

Abbie looked up at the lights and the twinkling stars of red and yellow and blue. 'Where did you find them?'

'In the garage. With a Christmas tree, a bunch of decorations and this.' He tapped the radio and grinned. 'Thought I'd do a little recycling. The Christmas tree's over there. I didn't have the heart to leave it out.'

Abbie followed his nod and her heart gave a jolt of surprise. A little green tree, unromantically synthetic and with some of its branches missing, stood propped in a large flowerpot. He'd wound a daisy or two into the faded glitter and curled a yellow rose on the top with a peg.

'I'd forgotten it,' she said, and cleared her throat. 'Cas, it's a lovely thought. Totally unexpected.' She glanced up at the lights. 'I'm just…speechless.'

'Another first.' He laughed, and she laughed, too. 'Drink?'

'Don't tell me it's champagne?'

His eyes were dark and very sexy as he arched an eyebrow. 'The late store didn't have luxuries. Just a cheap and probably undrinkable red.'

She followed him to the table and marvelled. A bottle of red wine, skewered vegetables, chicken and sausage and generously burned potatoes in their jackets overflowing with cheese and butter.

He poured her a glass then one for himself and chinked it against hers. 'You decide the toast,' he told her in a husky voice, and when something heartbreakingly soft and romantic began to weave its way shakily from the radio, she heard a brave voice reply.

'To us?'

'To us,' he repeated, looking into her eyes.

She gulped—far too quickly—far too inappropriately, because she didn't need wine. The expression written in his gaze was aphrodisiac enough.

CHAPTER ELEVEN

'AND then…' Abbie laughed, as she propped herself up on her elbow. 'Dad had made this half-hearted citizen's arrest…whilst he was trying to help the man into the car. But, of course, in climbing through the shop window, the thief had cut himself pretty badly. So Dad had to staunch the blood with a cloth Mrs James had given him—and by the time he got him to Casualty, the poor man could hardly move anyway…'

'And the story went down in village history.' Cas chuckled, nodding as he stretched beside her on the blanket. 'Yes, I've heard various versions. My favourite is the one by Mr James's grandson. Know it?'

Glowing with pride, Abbie shook her head. She wanted to hear every word—to listen to Cas all night, to lie here on the blanket, curled up under the fairy lights in the trees. It was so easy just to be with him, listen to him.

'The boy, who was only five at the time,' Cas continued, his laughter barely repressed, 'was staying for Christmas with his grandparents. The Jameses heard this almighty crash in their shop and went to investigate. The boy woke up and went into the shop to discover his grandparents and your father ''wrapping up'' the burglar. Mrs James, not wanting her grandson alarmed, explained it was Father Christmas who had taken an unfortunate detour on the way back to the North Pole. And the doctor was just making certain he was well enough to ride on his sleigh again.'

'You're joking?' Abbie gasped.

'Not at all. I heard it from the boy himself, now in his twenties. He came as a temporary resident to the surgery last summer.' Cas leaned back and laughed, unable to contain himself, and Abbie stroked the tears from her eyes.

'Your father was quite a man,' he sighed eventually, and grinned. 'I wish I'd known him longer.'

Abbie nodded, her smile wistful. 'I wish you had.'

'He was proud of you, Abbie,' he said, and she nodded.

'I just wish…' she began, then shrugged, looking down at the blanket and smoothing her hand over its thickness. 'No, I don't wish anything. Not really.'

'Don't have regrets. He wouldn't want that.' He reached out and curled a finger under her chin. 'Abbie…?'

She swallowed, her body trembling. Did Cas know what he was doing to her? How much she wanted him to touch her? Was he mind-reading again?

She looked up into a gaze that liquefied her body. The dark lashes fanned down on his cheeks and his eyes captured her reflection as they lay there, only inches apart. So close. She only had to reach out and touch him, lay her fingers lightly on his arm, to know that he would respond.

She felt it, sensed his closeness. The gulf between them had closed. She yearned to lean against him, to encircle him with her arms, tangle her fingers in his hair. If only she had the courage she'd do it…

'Come here,' he whispered.

She leaned towards him, felt the exquisite slide of his hand over her back and into her hair. It played there, drawing a murmur of ecstasy from her throat and a deep sigh from the hard cage of his ribs.

She let her hand lie lightly on his shoulder, testing her resolve. If this was going to be over in seconds…if this was just a fantasy…or a trick…or a wild excursion into a blissful summer night that was as brief as it was beautiful…

But it wasn't, and her resolve crumbled the moment she felt his hot skin under the shirt. And then somehow she was lying on the blanket, her body consumed by yearning. He was leaning over her, breathing in and exhaling so fiercely that their hearts fought for space. With a tiny moan, she eased herself into his shape and desire rippled through him.

So seductively.

So intoxicatingly. And passed into her. Under a sky that was created by heaven for love-making. She felt his breath on her cheek and over her face, and her hands explored every little muscle and curve that she'd only ever imagined before. Now she knew how he felt, how he breathed and now, as his lips covered hers, how he kissed.

This time it was a real kiss. Not like before on the stairs—that kiss seemed like a faded summer. This was something else. Something incredible…

'Abbie, I want you,' he groaned, and sucked in a tenuous breath until he felt her fingers trace the line of his mouth and she nodded.

'I want you, too.'

Then he drew her against him and fire leapt between their mouths and very slowly he tugged her up, hauling her into his arms.

And into the house.

It was like finding her way back home. To her true home. The one she had been away from for so long. The one she had always known existed. The make-believe land of fantasy, the garden of Eden.

She'd found the path and had followed its curves. And suddenly the gate she'd visualised was open and she walked through it, because being with Cas was the most wonderful thing in the world. The most familiar.

He matched her need with his, was tender and passionate, and his love-making seemed to fit around her like a glove. Touching all the right spots, soothing the lonely and sad places that she hadn't realised were still there. Lighting up her mind and body like a wake-up call that she had been missing all her life.

His arms were strong and his body was firm and wonderfully masculine. Every muscle seemed to shudder under her touch. And she touched every one. Almost disbelievingly. She fitted him so well. He seemed to know everything that pleased her. That made her a woman.

His hands were remarkable. Soft and teasing one moment. Seeking and needy the next, travelling over her body like a wind, then a breeze and then a soft, aching flutter. They aroused her and caressed, discovered and revealed. And all she heard was the little message singing in her head and heart.

I'm home.

And when it was over, or she thought it was over, he began again, as hungry for her as she was for him. Nothing to hide now, no inhibition or distrust. The moment of doubt was hers alone. A vague thought she should be taking precautions, but she didn't want to stop—couldn't bear to risk a single murmur that might break the spell. And there was always the morning-after pill…

And when a low rumble trickled from his throat and they lay, spent and linked between damp sheets and pounding hearts, she knew bliss.

'Abbie?' he murmured, lazily turning as the heat radiated off him. And she wriggled round as well and slid her arms around his neck and looked into the depths of his eyes.

'What?' She smiled and for answer he drew her against him and kissed her and the sigh that came from him felt as though it was her own. 'You're beautiful,' he muttered, the hitch in his voice making her shudder. 'You're a very beautiful, sexy woman.'

'Kiss me,' she told him. 'All I want you to do is kiss me.'

He bent his head and kissed her, the fire still burning on his lips. He laid his cheek against hers and cupped her breast with tender fingers. 'I've lain here at nights and wondered,' he whispered softly into her ear. 'Wondered what you were thinking, with just a ceiling between us. You down there and me up here. And whether you were wondering the same thing.'

Abbie arched against him and closed her eyes at his touch. 'I thought you could read my mind.'

Cas took a breath and his fingers trickled over the alert pink bud in a way that caused sparks flying down her spine. 'I didn't think I'd ever have you in bed beside me.'

'That's not the answer I wanted.'

'I know. But it will have to do.' He pulled her down into the bed and laid his knee on her thigh, trapping her, so that she gave a token protest as he tugged her against him. 'I don't want to answer any more questions. Or think of the morning. Or tomorrow. Or next week. I just want the here and now. And you.'

Words that she found achingly touching as he kissed her. But frightening, too. Because there was always tomorrow. And she feared he was a man of his word.

Abbie woke to a feeling of utter bliss. Her body floating on a cloud. Or on the crest of a fluffy blue ocean. Or on an eiderdown of feathers. She could be anywhere in her heaven and, snaking out her hand, she moaned deliciously and slowly opened her eyes.

She was alone. Cas's side of the bed was rumpled and the window was wide open, as though he'd been standing there. His little clock on the bedside cabinet said a quarter past seven and she slithered from the sheets, wondering if it all had been another incredible dream.

But it hadn't been, because this was his bed. And she remembered quite clearly falling into it. With her arms around his neck. And her body on fire.

She saw her clothes piled neatly on the chair and debated whether to put them on. But there was a towelling robe behind the door and she grabbed it. Then she tiptoed to the bathroom and pushed open the door.

His smell. His shaver on the side. A towel had been used and the tap was dripping slightly. She twirled it, retraced her steps and claimed her clothes. The landing and stairs were quiet. And she stood and listened outside her room.

The house seemed oddly quiet. She couldn't smell anything either. No coffee or bacon, so the kitchen wasn't in use.

He was probably in the office or surgery. It was Monday and she had open surgery this morning. Cas had calls and…

And what?

She only wanted to think about last night. Savour the memory, bring back his words and his touch. Back in her own room she twirled her hair on top of her head and slid under the shower. Lifted her face and closed her eyes. She remembered every second. Laughing and talking as though they'd known each other a lifetime. The sky full of silver and the trees twinkling with gems. The food and the wine—though she hadn't needed wine to help her relax. Caspar had made her feel totally at ease.

They had drunk from a natural magic. His body beside her, the low rumble that erupted from his throat. His touch. His tenderness and passion and his *knowing*. She had never been loved so entirely, as though he had known every part of her instinctually.

She left the shower, pampered herself, preened a little in the mirror and reluctantly put on her working clothes—a fresh white blouse and slim navy skirt. And bundled her damp hair into a band. Most of the curls were captured and she settled on leaving it without pins or persuasion.

Her eyes, though, she could do nothing about. Greener than ever before with little black orbs as centres that glowed seductively. She recognised a satisfied woman, a woman at one with herself. And a smile flickered on her lips.

She'd been right. Cas wasn't in the kitchen and he wasn't in the office. So when she pushed open the door to the surgery, she wasn't surprised to see him sitting there, head down, eyes fixed intently on the notes in front of him.

He was dressed in a light grey polo shirt, and the short sleeves and slightly open neck made him look deliciously sexy. Whorls of black hair crept over his arms and down to his wrists. His hair was growing again, curling over his collar. Somehow she related the short style to Venetia. And at that moment she wasn't even going to think the name inside her head!

But Abbie couldn't help wondering what Cas was feeling about Venetia. How serious was the relationship between them? And if they were lovers, was he already having regrets about last night?

The pangs of jealousy that she always felt when she thought of Venetia were now mixed with guilt. And yet Cas had made love to her and told her he wanted her. And even though he might not have meant what he'd said, Abbie wanted to believe it was true.

'Hi,' she said, and he looked up.

His dark eyes were an unfathomable brown that could, she always thought, be black. 'Hi,' he said, and something in his voice had changed.

'Sleep well?' She slid down into the patient's chair, ignoring the loathsome little niggle of doubt. Her eyes were greedy for everything. Recalling everything. Wanting it all over again.

'Until around six, yes,' he told her, and leaned back in the chair.

'I didn't hear you get up,' she murmured softly, wondering if she had the courage to reach across and open those two little buttons on the top of his shirt.

'The phone rang. We had a call—or rather *you* did.'

Abbie's smile faded as she sat up slowly. 'A call for me, at that time in the morning?'

'I didn't wake you. Maybe I should have done. But he was having breakfast anyway…'

'*He?*' she repeated, her brow furrowed.

Cas stared at her and leaned back in his chair. 'Your friend—Jon Kirk.'

'Jon?' Abbie replied bewilderedly. 'What did he want?'

Cas steepled his fingers and leaned his elbows on the arms of the chair. 'You.'

She felt a shiver thread over her spine as she gazed at him. 'Cas, I mean, what did he want to say? Did he leave a message?'

He nodded slowly, unfolded himself and ripped a page from the notebook. He fluttered it in front of her on the desk. 'He's in London. Heathrow. And he's coming down to Tilly today. I said you'd ring that number around eight.'

Abbie half laughed. 'But he can't be. The arrangement when we last spoke was that I'd meet him for lunch in London.'

'He's obviously changed his mind.' Cas cut her short as he stood up and hauled his case from behind the desk.

'Don't go yet,' she pleaded, a hitch in her voice.

He gave her a puzzled frown, then in a voice that was as remote as his expression he muttered, 'What is there to say?'

'But, Cas, last night—' she began, but he flayed her with reproachful eyes.

'It was a mistake, Abbie,' he told her as he walked to the door. 'And we both know it. You'd better make that call—and forget that last night ever happened.'

She felt sick and wretched and desperate. Why had he said that? She couldn't believe he had. Last night she had felt part of him, had reached inside him—she'd thought. They had gone to sleep in each other's arms, lovingly, tenderly. Yet this morning he'd told her it had been a mistake.

She stared at the scrawled message, then lifted the telephone. She didn't want to make this call, but she had better get it over with. She would have to think about Cas later. Try to work out what had happened and deal with priorities.

First Jon.

Then the surgery.

Then…somehow she had to speak to Cas. To try to find a way past that brick wall. She dialled the number and heard Jon's voice. Once upon a time, she would have been warmed by his American drawl, his soft good humour and intelligence. Now she found herself thinking that he couldn't have arrived in her life at a more inopportune time.

'Abbie!' He was delighted to hear her and she relented slightly.

'Jon—you're in England.'

'I am, honey. A little earlier than planned. My vacation's extended and I can't wait to see you.'

'Cas said you were thinking about coming to Tilly—'

'Not thinking, Abbie, on my way. Will you be around later today?'

She felt trapped. What could she say? 'Yes, but, Jon—'

'Don't worry about meeting me. I'll find my way there. Honey, I've missed you. We all missed you. I've come to take you home.'

Abbie froze. 'Jon—' she began, but had to stop as the static grew louder and Jon's voice broke up. All she heard was, 'Catch you soon.'

And he was gone.

It wasn't the easiest morning of Abbie's life. For once she wished there were no patients and she could try to think out what Jon might have said during the call. Cas had changed since last night. And it could only be Jon—so what had been spoken about? But other than a stab at a few irrational thoughts, she came up with nothing.

Susan Dunning was the first to arrive at the surgery, accompanied by little Joanne. Susan pushed the buggy into the surgery and sat down, lifting the baby onto her lap. 'I thought you'd

like to know,' she said quietly, rocking the baby
in her arms, 'that I've made a few decisions
about my life and Joanne's. What you and Dr
Darke said made an impression. And I know that
I've got to stand on my own feet. I've applied to
the council for a flat for Joanne and me. If our
circumstances meet their criteria, I'll go on a list.
All the council properties in the village are quite
nice, so it will be worth the wait.'

'That's good news, Susan. Have you told your
dad?'

'Yes, and Aunt Marjorie.'

Abbie raised her eyebrows. 'What was their
reaction?'

Susan chuckled softly. 'Can't you imagine?
Aunt Marjorie said I couldn't cope at home, so
how was I going to cope on my own. And Dad
didn't say much at all, until I said that when
Mum was discharged it would be easier all round
if we weren't there.'

'And what about Joanne?' Abbie glanced
down at the contented infant. 'How is she?'

'As you can see, much better,' Susan replied,
replacing Joanne in the buggy. 'It's strange, but
since the school episode a lot's changed. I don't
mind admitting I was scared stiff in that cupboard, but not for myself—for Joanne. I told myself if we got out OK, I'd never do any more

complaining about anything or anyone. I realised it's only me who can make a change in my life.'

'It's a hard lesson to learn,' Abbie said sympathetically. 'But you seem happier, Sue, now you've decided to do something positive.'

Susan nodded. 'Joanne's actually slept through the night twice now.'

'Because she knows you're feeling better.' Abbie smiled as Joanne gurgled.

'It's as if we both came out of the school cupboard different people.' Susan laughed. 'Daft or what? Anyway, we must go.' She stood up and paused. 'And there's something else,' she added, and blushed. 'I've written to Ralf, care of his sister, and told him about Joanne.'

Abbie nodded slowly. 'What made you decide to tell him?'

'Well, I thought about what you and Dr Darke said. Joanne has a right to know her own father. My dad and me don't always see eye to eye, but I wouldn't like to be without him. What am I going to say to Joanne if she asks me why I never told him? And it's inevitable she will. At least I'll have no regrets this way, no matter what Ralf decides to do. Ignore me, or reply—it'll be his choice.'

'I hope he'll reply.' Abbie smiled. 'In fact, I think he will.'

Susan grinned. 'Bit of a shock, knowing you're a dad all of a sudden.'

Abbie watched Susan bend to gently tug the little sun hat into place and steer the buggy out of the surgery. As there was no one waiting, she strolled with her onto the drive and they glanced at the hedge behind which they could hear the noise of the workmen.

'Won't be long before it's finished, will it?' Susan asked. 'What's it going to be called, this poly…?'

'Polyclinic,' Abbie said. 'I don't know what plans Dr Darke has for the name.'

'Will you be staying open at Tilly House?' Susan frowned.

'No, I'm selling the property,' Abbie admitted, knowing that it was probably already common knowledge in the village.

Susan didn't look surprised. Instead, she gave the house a thoughtful glance. 'Well, it'll be the end of an era. Your dad brought me and my sisters into this world. But I reckon if there's anyone that can fill your father's shoes, it's Dr Darke.' Quickly casting her gaze at Abbie, she bit her lip. 'Oh, there I go again, putting my foot in it. I didn't mean that you, his daughter, couldn't. I just meant what with you off on your adventures round the world…'

'It's all right, Sue,' Abbie said. 'You're right. Dr Darke is a wonderful doctor.'

'And a good man, if you ask me,' Susan added. 'He's got his heart in the right place. And he'll make some lucky woman a fantastic husband one day. But, then, of course,' she said slowly, arching an eyebrow at Abbie, 'you don't need me to tell you that.'

Abbie finished her open surgery and looked at the clock. Just after one. Cas hadn't returned from his calls and since Charlie was busy finishing the filing she felt at a loose end.

Where was Jon? And, more importantly, what was she going to do with him when he arrived? Susan's comment still taunted her. Were her feelings for Cas so apparent? Or had Susan just struck lucky with that remark? Their conversation had unsettled Abbie, not least Susan's remarks about Cas being the one to replace her father, and Cas having his heart in the right place. If ever she'd distrusted Cas, she realised now that she should have known better.

Dad had trusted him. And that should have been good enough. Instead, she'd struggled every inch of the way with their relationship. Until last night when he'd made love to her and her universe had changed.

'All done,' Charlie said, coming out of the office and smiling. 'There's a couple of files I can't find in the carousel. But they can wait until tomorrow if you're off somewhere.'

Abbie realised she was standing in the hall and staring out of the open front door. 'No, I'm not, Charlie. But you go. Make the most of the sunshine.'

Charlie grinned under her colourful braids. 'Well, if it's all right, I will go a bit early. I'm taking Nanna out to tea this afternoon. I've ordered a taxi and we're going into Tilly.'

'I'll gift you a lift in that case,' Abbie offered. 'I've no one else to see.'

'Are you sure?'

Abbie nodded and wondered as they walked to the car whether Jon might phone whilst she was away. Unhelpfully, the thought of Jon's arrival dismayed her. Only a few weeks ago she would have welcomed his visit. Yearned for news of her colleagues and friends. And been flattered by his teasing comment about taking her back to the States.

But not now. Not since last night.

As she jumped in the car beside Charlie, she caught herself wishing she could turn back the clock. To yesterday and a sky filled with stars and fairy lights, curled up on a blanket on the ground.

CHAPTER TWELVE

JON eventually rang that evening, announcing the loss of his luggage. He was attempting to recover it, but it could take hours and he couldn't come without it.

Abbie's nerves were stretched. She hadn't seen Cas all day and when he had returned at four, he'd said he didn't have time to stop. He'd be in the field next door if he was needed.

'Great,' Abbie had muttered as his long, lean figure, clad in vest and jeans, had hurtled down the drive. 'Thanks for your time.' But he hadn't caught her sarcasm. He'd just disappeared and all she'd glimpsed of him over the hedge had been the tip of the hard yellow hat.

What he was doing there until dark, she couldn't think. And she wasn't going to beg for attention. And when he came in and she was in bed, she listened to his footsteps on the stairs, then the soft pad across the floor above her.

And she trembled at the memory of his remark about her being down here and him up there. And tortured herself even more. She couldn't sleep.

She felt her body crying out to him. Defeated, the tears fell and soaked her pillow.

She wanted him so much. Why had he told her their love-making had been a mistake? He was the best thing that had ever happened to her. And she wanted to tell him.

But she couldn't.

She was stuck with the heartache. And her pride.

And another day, waiting for Jon.

A slimline Howard Bailey swaggered into surgery the following morning and made an announcement.

'I'm off to Disneyland in three weeks, Doc,' he told Abbie. 'With my daughter, her husband and the two grandchildren. I'm going to enjoy a fortnight of unadulterated fun.'

'Sounds gorgeous,' Abbie said approvingly. 'And you're looking very slim. How are you feeling?'

'A heck of a lot better than I was three months ago, that's for sure,' Howard told her with relief. 'I wouldn't be going on this little jaunt if I wasn't.'

'And you've had your check with the consultant?' Abbie prompted.

'Last week. He said I'm looking good, but I'll probably fare better watching the kids, rather than outdoing them on the rides.'

Abbie nodded. 'Your heart valve replacement operation was just a year ago, so perhaps, even though you're fit and well now, it would be a good idea to bear his advice in mind.'

Howard nodded slowly. 'I thought that first valve I had put in four years ago would last for ever. Until your dad told me the device wasn't working properly.'

'Some valves need repairing or replacing,' Abbie agreed. 'The surgeon didn't know for sure until he examined the old one during your last op. He decided on a new device, sutured a mechanical valve into position and closed the aorta. Your recent weight loss will help to sustain your good health, so keep it up.'

'That's why I'm keeping to my diet,' Howard agreed firmly. 'Now, what I want to know is, if I do feel a bit cranky on holiday, can I rely on the medical bods over there? I know you work in the States and treat all these glamorous stars. Is it only them that have the best of attention, or am I going to end up like one of these ER casualties that you see on TV?'

Abbie found herself repressing a smile. What would Howard think if he knew exactly in which area she worked? 'In the first place, I don't think you'll see the inside of an American hospital,' she assured him. 'The consultant wouldn't let you go if he thought there was a risk. In the second place, I've never treated anyone famous, so I can only advise you to have a good insurance, take all your medication and the details of your condition should an emergency arise.'

Howard threw her a teasing glance. 'I thought I was going to get a bit of gossip to flaunt on the plane.'

'Sorry I can't oblige.' Abbie laughed. 'But you can tell me all about Disneyland when you come back.'

'It's a date,' he nodded, standing up and walking to the door. 'See you in September.'

'I hope so,' Abbie replied, then frowned. 'Though I'm flying back myself then.'

'So soon?' Howard's face dropped.

Abbie was about to respond when she heard voices in the hall. Her gaze flickered to the door and Howard opened it. Outside stood the tall figure of Cas, who Abbie had assumed was out on his calls but evidently wasn't. With him was a slightly smaller, fair-haired man, with two large navy blue suitcases at his side.

Howard saw Cas and went out to join him. Before Abbie could move from her seat Jon was striding into the surgery. She was halfway up when he thrust the case he was carrying down beside her desk and hauled her into his arms.

'Abbie, honey!' She caught her breath as she was engulfed in a bear hug of an embrace. He held her against him and she met Cas's eyes over his shoulder. Though Cas was talking to Howard, his gaze locked with hers. She was trapped as she laid her hands on Jon's waist and his mouth came down to kiss her. She managed to turn her face slightly and his mouth brushed her cheek.

When she looked back into the hall Cas had turned away and was lugging a second blue case up the stairs.

'I saw Buckingham Palace and the Tower of London,' Jon said between forkfuls of pasta, 'praying that the guys at the airport would turn up my stuff. And they did. Kinda gave me time to see the sights. I would have loved you guys with me to show me around, though.'

They were eating in the kitchen and Abbie had made the best she could of what there was in the fridge. She hadn't imagined in her wildest dreams that they would be acting as hosts to Jon. She glanced at Cas across the table. He was listening to Jon and had so far managed to avoid her questioning glance.

'It was really great, bumping into you like that,' Jon was saying, his vivid blue eyes and handsome face exactly as she recalled. Despite his high quota of stunning intelligence, he rarely came over in company as the brilliant researcher he was. That was what had attracted her in the early days. Before she'd realised it was what attracted every other female in the vicinity.

Jon Kirk was a married man. Married to his ambition. But that still didn't stop women falling for him. A smile touched Abbie's lips as she watched him eat energetically. Slim and lean, he was a health fanatic. And he had the body to prove it. Wearing a flawlessly uncreased jogging top and muscle-hugging shorts, she thought how he looked more like one of Howard's celebs than a highly regarded medical researcher.

Why was he here? she wondered absently. Why hadn't he stuck to their arrangement of meeting her briefly in London?

'How did you know it was Cas?' Abbie asked, trying to ignore the irritation she felt at his sudden appearance.

'I didn't. Cas found me.' Jon shrugged 'There I was, standing in the…what do you call it, Cas?'

'Market-place.'

'Yeah, market-place. He heard me asking directions from one of those little guys that do the traffic thing?'

'The traffic warden,' Cas clarified, and flicked her a glance. 'I'd just made a call at the tea-rooms. Gilli had another faint customer.'

'And this wonderful man hears my accent,' Jon continued delightedly, 'and comes over and says who he is.'

Abbie looked at Cas and raised her eyebrows. 'And it was then you tried the King's Head?'

'Quaint little place,' Jon interrupted, gulping pasta, 'but all booked up.' He popped the last bit into his mouth. 'Then Cas said you'd rustle up a bed here, no problem.' He dabbed his mouth with a napkin. 'So we went for a…' He lifted his glass and waved it in front of Cas's face.

'A pint,' Cas said, 'at The Crow.'

'And a pie.' Abbie was unable to smother the sarcasm.

'Yeah, great pies.' Jon nodded. 'And great conversation.'

'Yes,' Cas agreed in an altogether different tone of voice. Levelled at her, it had the crispness of a frosty morning. 'We caught up on transatlantic news.'

Abbie looked at Cas and pushed her plate away. The pasta was delicious but she was beginning to feel queasy. 'What sort of news?'

'I told Cas all about our work,' Jon gushed with energy. 'The clinic, Abbie, is doing great. We've got new sponsorship and a higher profile. That means we've got one great future ahead of us.'

Abbie felt the knot tighten in her stomach. 'The clinic,' she murmured.

'Yes, the rehabilitation clinic and all its good work,' Cas said with eyes that glittered coldly.

Abbie couldn't hide the deep flush that rose up her throat. She glanced at Jon, who was obviously unaware that until today Cas had had absolutely no idea of her life and career in the States. And was, no doubt, adding the fatal error of her double life to her scoresheet of sins.

Jon seemed every bit as energetic as he was five hours previously. When would he go to bed? And, more importantly, when would she ever have the chance to be alone with Cas?

'I've put you in the spare room next to Cas,' Abbie said as she stretched her legs and stifled a yawn. The lounge was muggy, even with the window open, and the moths were circling, attracted by the light. 'There are towels beside the bed in the cupboard. If there's anything you want, just let me know.'

'I dumped your cases by your door,' Cas said, prising himself up from the armchair. A solid evening of listening to Jon and his wonderful but exhausting liturgy on medical research had left Abbie feeling drained. And she saw that Cas, polite as he had been, looked appallingly tired.

She wanted to hold him, to soothe the deep furrows from his forehead and the tiny, sexy lines at the corners of his eyes. She wanted to slide against him, run her fingers over that hard ripple of abdomen that had her gulping down air in lungfuls and lose herself in his arms. Basically, she wanted to crawl into his bed and sleep all night beside him. And her eyes must have held a glimmer of lust because she caught Jon staring at her oddly.

'I'll come up with you and check you've everything,' she said quickly, avoiding his stare.

'Heck, I hope I don't get under your feet this week.' He grinned. 'Just yell at me if I do.'

This week? Abbie's heart sank. He was going to stay all week? She looked at Cas, but he was already making his exit.

'Sure is a quaint old place,' Jon was saying as he followed her up the stairs. 'You never told me about any of this.'

Abbie hurried on past her own floor and up the next flight. 'No, well, these old houses aren't uncommon in England.'

'But this has character.' Jon was behind her as she passed Cas's door and came to a halt at the next one.

'The bathroom's at the end,' she told him, and glanced down at the luggage. 'How long did you say you were staying in England, Jon?'

'Oh, long enough to convince you to come home with me.' Suddenly he reached out and drew her into his arms. 'Abbie, I've missed you.'

'Jon—I don't know what to say,' she fumbled. She couldn't believe this was happening.

'Don't say anything. Can I come with you to-morrow?'

'Where?' She laid her hands on his chest and realised she was trapped.

'On your calls—anywhere. I want to be with you. Know what you do. Understand your work.' His face was coming down closer and she realised he was going to kiss her.

'Jon, no.'

Just then a creak on the stairs made them turn. Jon's hands were still on her arms as Cas rounded the corner.

'Sorry,' Cas grunted, yanking at the handle of his door. His gaze briefly tangled with Abbie's and she strangled a groan in her throat. Then he shot inside and the door closed with a thud.

'He's a nice guy,' Jon said, trying to fold her back into his arms. 'Now, where did we get to?'

'You'd better get some sleep,' she told him, pushing away and praying he wouldn't hold onto her or she'd have to make a scene. Then she was heading along the hallway, aching to stop at Cas's door, almost running on down the landing and stairs, her heart banging like a drum.

'See you in the morning, honey,' he called after her.

Abbie closed her bedroom door and leaned against it, her long lashes flicking wetly down on her cheeks. They were tears of anger and resentment and confusion. OK, she might have got some things wrong. Jon had suddenly appeared on the scene, but then so had Venetia.

And she hadn't gone off in a huff when Cas had stayed out with Venetia. She plonked herself down on her bed and angrily swiped at her tears.

Correction. She had been in a bit of a huff.

But, then, she'd had to play gooseberry for a whole evening at the King's Head. And anyway, they'd got over all that and survived the flu outbreak and found Susan Dunning and...

Abbie sank back on the bed and stared up at the ceiling. She was rambling. She was upset.

And she couldn't hold all her thoughts together. She struggled to calm herself but it didn't work. She kept getting images of him, lying directly above her, his long, lean body tangled in the sheets. Was he thinking of her? Did he know how much she missed him?

Why wouldn't he speak to her? Why weren't they together now, curled up in each other's arms?

'Damn it,' she spluttered, sitting up. 'I'm going to drive myself crazy like this.' She yanked her bag onto the bed and found her mobile. This was as good a way as any. Not as satisfying as hammering on his door. But with Jon in the next room she could hardly do that.

She stabbed his number and waited.

'Yes?'

'It's me.'

'What is it, Abbie?'

'I think we should talk.'

'At this time of night?'

She glanced at her travel clock. 'It's not late. Not really. I'll meet you in the kitchen.'

'Abbie, this is—'

She jabbed the button and slid the phone triumphantly back into her bag. Then she panicked. What was she going to say?

'Exactly what you've been saying to yourself, idiot,' she muttered, and went to the mirror. Two large, puzzled green eyes stared out under a cascade of dark auburn hair. She thought the pale face looked lost and wistful and not in the least seductive.

She allowed him five minutes, then opened her door. There was no noise from the floor above and she tiptoed downstairs, praying Jon was asleep.

When she got to the kitchen the light was on and Cas was waiting, leaning against the sink, muscled arms folded. He looked thunderous, and she swallowed. If she could have safely let her eyes linger on his gorgeous, tanned body—wonderfully bereft of clothes, just a vest and a pair of shorts that he'd obviously tugged on for decency's sake—she would have. But she was too scared she'd forget everything and melt into a puddle at his feet instead.

So she tossed back her hair, pulled out a stool and sat down. Maintaining his stare was difficult, but not impossible. Difficult, because his eyes were as angry as her own and she preferred that to indifference.

'Aren't you going to sit down?'

'Will this take long?' He arched his eyebrows.

'No. But I'm getting a pain in my neck looking up.'

He didn't sigh, but did something close enough and sprawled into a chair, leaning his arms on the table. They were such sexy arms, so dark and muscled and strong. With lovely fingers that had made their night in bed so seductive and special and—

'Abbie. I'm tired. You're tired. Say what you have to say. Then we can go to bed.'

'I'm not tired. I'm confused. I just don't understand—'

He harrumphed loudly. '*You* don't understand? That's rich.'

'All right, then. Tell me what you don't understand.'

'How long have you got?'

'Funny.'

'Abbie—I just saw you kissing the guy!'

She couldn't believe she'd just heard that. 'I wasn't kissing him.'

'And why the lies?' he demanded, ignoring her. 'Why not tell me about the clinic you work for?'

'I would have,' she spluttered. 'You never actually asked. You just assumed I was working at the hospital I'd gone to when I left England.'

'So when did this great conversion to work for humanity's sake take place? When you met Jon Kirk, I suppose.'

'No,' she answered, hurt at his sarcasm. 'Well, when I met him, yes, but it wasn't because of Jon—'

'That your whole life changed,' he finished for her. 'That you couldn't come home to see your father?'

'That's not true,' she said, and held back the tears. 'Jon was responsible for a lot of good in my life and I wanted to tell Dad about him.'

'So you admit Jon means that much to you?' he slammed at her. 'What is it, Abbie, the glamour and the celebrity status you crave?' He laughed shortly. 'Well, you're certainly heading in the right direction. That guy came all the way over here just for you. Some compliment eh?'

'Cas, you're not listening. It's not like that.'

He pushed back the chair and stared down at her. In his eyes she saw pain and hurt as well as anger, and his voice was shaking when he spoke. 'Abbie I can overlook you not telling me about your life. It's yours. It's personal. I can even understand you sleeping with me in a moment of— what shall we call it? Abandon. But what I can't forgive is how you had the nerve to accuse me of befriending your father and stealing his land.

My God, you called me an opportunist, but if there was ever an opportunist on this earth, I'm looking right at her.'

He all but snarled, thrust a hand like a whip through his hair and trod noisily out of the kitchen. Abbie sat still, waiting for her pounding heart to slow down so that she could breathe.

She wanted to cry, but she couldn't. She wanted to scream at him and tell him that he had no right to say those things. That she hadn't slept with him in a moment of abandon and that he was completely wrong about Jon. And most of all, she wanted to say that she hadn't ever called him an opportunist.

But the dreadful thing was—she had.

She could barely believe it herself. But she had. And she supposed there was no use in wishing she hadn't. She couldn't put right the past. She couldn't even put right the present. And sure as eggs were eggs, she knew now she hadn't any hope of making right her future.

At least, not with Cas.

CHAPTER THIRTEEN

IT WASN'T until a few days later that Abbie realised she had forgotten to take the morning-after
pill. It was an omission that she tried to justify
because of her quarrel with Cas and Jon's sudden
arrival putting everything out of her mind. But
as the day wore on, whatever had caused the
memory slip seemed almost unimportant. It was
done and she could only hope that her period
would arrive. She put the worry to the back of
her mind as she worked her way through open
surgery.

She had managed to persuade Jon to satisfy
his curiosity about the polyclinic. 'See it for
yourself,' she'd told him at breakfast when Cas
had been noticeably absent.

'Sure will,' Jon had agreed eagerly. 'And this
afternoon I'll come back for you.'

'I might still be working,' she'd protested.

'OK, honey. Then I'll just hang out for a while
till you're finished.'

Abbie had nodded and tried a smile, but it had
cost her dearly. The thought of his presence for

the whole week was disturbing enough, her work the only valid excuse for her personal space.

After open surgery was over, though, he was back. Tanned and wearing a T-shirt, he was waiting for her in the garden.

'So what did you think of the building?' she asked him.

'Great. Cas showed me around when he came back from his calls.'

'Oh.' She swallowed on the injustice. 'That's nice.' Cas had time to show off his polyclinic, but not a moment to share with her.

'Show me the beach, Abbie,' Jon implored her.

'I have prescriptions to write,' she stalled, praying for a miracle—like a sudden typhoon or mini-tidal wave. 'And I want to help Charlie with some filing—'

'It'll keep, won't it?' Jon looked abandoned. 'I want to see this wonderful British coastline of yours.'

Eventually she gave in and packed a picnic and they walked down to the beach and swam off the little coves. But she kept remembering her swim with Cas and the look of his sleek, wet body as they'd lain on the sand and watched the surf roll in.

She tried her best to be good company. But when Jon said how much he'd missed her and tried to kiss her, she turned her head and moved out of his reach. When they arrived home, he trapped her hand as they stood in the hall. 'I'll take you out to dinner,' he decided. 'You look too pretty to cook.'

'No—' she began as Cas came down the stairs and saw them standing together.

'See you later,' he said, hunching his shoulders as he passed. 'I'm off to The Crow. Greg's taking calls.'

'What about supper?' she asked as a trail of something achingly gorgeous wafted behind him. She inhaled it as though she were starving.

'I'm eating out,' he called, not bothering to look back.

'Hey, Cas, wanna eat with us?' Jon yelled.

But Cas didn't hear. They watched him jump into the four-wheel-drive and accelerate away down the track.

'Nice guy,' Jon commented, sliding his hand around her waist. 'I like him.'

And so they went out to dinner. They used her car and found a country pub where the sun streamed in through lattice windows. Jon turned every woman's head, yet he seemed to have eyes only for her.

Abbie managed to get through the meal, then claimed a headache.

'So it's home?' Jon asked disappointedly.

'It's been lovely,' she lied.

The house was in darkness when they returned and she wondered where Cas was. 'Abbie—' Jon began as she switched on the lights.

'I really do have an awful headache,' she said, and scrambled for the stairs.

'Aw, Abbie, don't leave me.' He stood, his blue eyes reproving her. 'You know how I feel about you.'

She sighed softly. 'Jon, you're a wonderful man and a brilliant doctor. And we were friends in the States and we're friends here. But there's never been anything more between us.'

'You English,' he murmured. 'So polite.'

'Sleep well,' she said, and headed up the stairs. He didn't follow her, but before she went to bed she slid the lock on the door.

And that was the way the week continued, Jon dogging her footsteps and Cas becoming invisible. She prayed for an epidemic, but mostly it was coughs and colds and a few odd bugs. Cas grudgingly offered to take Jon on his calls on Thursday, but only because Jon virtually invited himself. On Friday morning, after open surgery, she grasped the opportunity to drive Charlie home.

'I could have walked,' Charlie said as they hurtled along the lane. 'You needn't have bothered. Dr Kirk seemed disappointed you had to leave.'

'I'd like to see your grandmother,' Abbie said, and hoped she sounded convincing. She did want to see Eve, of course, but Charlie was smiling softly and she wondered what was going on under those beaded braids.

Eve, as always, made her welcome. 'Abbie, dear, how good to see you. Let's sit down in the lounge whilst Charlie makes us some tea.'

'How are you?' Abbie asked, sinking into the comfortable sofa, feeling more at home here than at Tilly House. Her gaze moved fondly round the room as Eve told her how much better she'd been of late. Charlie brought them tea and scones and then went into the garden to laze in the hammock and listen to her Walkman.

'Did Charlie tell you she's going back to college?' Eve asked. 'To study for a degree?'

'No—that's wonderful.' Abbie put down her tea cup. 'In September?'

Eve nodded. 'Thanks to you and Dr Darke.'

'I'm certain Charlie would have found her way. She's a very bright young woman.'

Eve nodded slowly. 'And so are you, my dear. Though I don't think I've ever seen you looking quite so…distracted.' She arched a delicate eyebrow. 'You know, I've known you since you were small, Abbie, and consider myself to be a close family friend as well as a patient. Bearing this in mind, is there any way I can be of help?'

Abbie dredged up a smile. 'I'm fine—really.'

But Eve knew her too well. 'Tell me to mind my business if you wish, but talking really does help, you know. Or am I too old to be of use?'

Abbie knew she wasn't going to win either way. So she found herself talking about Cas and just how passionate he was about the polyclinic. And equally how she, too, had once been focused on her career in the States. But as she spoke it became clear to her that her life had taken a different course since her return to England and would never be the same again after knowing Cas.

'Do you love him, Abbie?' Eve asked at last.

There was only one answer and she gave it as honestly as she could. 'Yes,' she confessed. 'Though we always seem to rub each other up the wrong way. From the moment we met.'

Eve smiled. 'Frederick and I were the same. In our early days you would never have thought we would make a year—let alone fifty together.

But once the sparks of our quarrels fizzled out, it was wonderful making up.'

Abbie was wondering if she and Cas would ever have the same opportunity. More than anything she wanted to spend a lifetime with Cas, but how could she? She wouldn't want him to stay with her for the baby's sake if she was pregnant, and that's what might happen if he discovered that she was carrying his child. The chances were he would feel duty bound to care for her and the baby. But he'd never told her he loved her. And she was old-fashioned enough to believe that being in love was the only reason that two people should remain together for the rest of their lives.

Just then Charlie returned from the garden, slipping off her earphones and smiling. 'More tea?' she asked, but Abbie shook her head and stood up.

'I must be going.'

'Give my love to that young man.' Eve smiled as she leaned forward and kissed Abbie on the cheek.

But she couldn't tell Cas anything when she arrived back. He'd left a message on the desk saying he'd made all the outstanding calls and that she shouldn't expect him back that night.

He was driving up to London.

*　　*　　*

The phone rang at nine the next morning. She was sitting in the office, wondering if Jon was up, when the phone rang.

'Hi.'

As greetings went it was pretty lame. 'Thank you for your note,' she said in the same monotone—and waited.

'Anything urgent come up?'

Only the small matter of our relationship, she wanted to reply. Or more accurately—and in his words—*their mistake*. Well, the *mistake* was growing into a catastrophe. She'd missed a period, one missed period wasn't conclusive—as she had been under a lot of stress—but she didn't want to think of the implications if she was pregnant. She'd *have* to take a test.

'Nothing urgent.' Wonderful!

'Good. Well, if that's the case, I won't hurry back. Greg's still taking calls, so you won't have to worry about tonight.'

'I changed it,' she told him. 'It's back to us for the weekend.'

'But why do that? It's Saturday. And you'll have to stay in.'

'I had no plans to go out,' she said, and lapsed into silence.

'Well, if that's what you want...'

No, it's not what I want, she hurled at him silently. I don't want to be here without you. I want you in my arms and if humanly possible I want to be in your bed where I can snuggle up to your beautiful body and know what it is to be in paradise again.

But he obviously wasn't in mind-reading mode. 'How's Jon?' he asked, and she stifled the urge to hang up.

'Fine.' She paused. 'How's Venetia?'

That is why you're there, isn't it? Don't try to deny it. Having Jon arrive has got you nicely off the hook, hasn't it?

'Last time I saw her, she was fine.'

'Good.'

'Well, see you tomorrow, then.'

'Yes. See you.'

Abbie thrust down the phone and glared at it. *Last time I saw her* indeed! Like ten minutes ago, in bed, no doubt. He had to be calling from Venetia's place. Abbie dialled one four seven one and felt ridiculous as the impersonal voice read back a mobile number.

A creak came from the stairs and Abbie looked up. 'Jon!'

He shrugged and leaned against the door. 'Gets kinda lonely in this old big house.'

She sighed. 'I'm not a very good host, am I?'

'Was that Cas on the phone?' he asked, and came and perched a thigh on her desk.

She nodded. 'He's staying in London.'

Jon met her gaze, then grinned. 'Are you and he…?'

Abbie blushed as his eyes tracked over her face. Before she could reply, he lifted his shoulders in a shrug. 'Hey, it's OK, Abbie. I crashed in on your scene, not the other way round.' He inclined his head and expelled a breath. 'You know, I think it's time I moved on. Look up some friends, see a few more sights.'

'You don't have to go,' she protested, feeling guilty.

'Guess my timing was all wrong.' He smiled. 'But maybe when you come home…?'

She didn't answer. Couldn't answer. Because she suddenly realised what her heart had been telling her for weeks. LA wasn't home.

'Sorry I couldn't stop to show you over yesterday,' Abbie apologised as the estate agent stood up. 'I had to take my friend to the station.'

The young man in the smart grey suit smiled. 'It was Sunday—and just a chance visit. Anyway, I showed them over whilst you were gone and they loved it.'

'They did?'

'They want to turn Tilly House into a commercial venture and propose quite a few changes. Total transformation by the sound of it. The location for a health spa is perfect,' he told her as they walked out to his car. 'I'll ring as soon as we have their offer.'

When he had driven off, Abbie's gaze ran fondly over Tilly House, at the elderly gables and bulging eaves and the wilderness of a garden. A health spa. Total transformation. The words jangled unpleasantly in her mind as she went back into the house.

Cas glanced up from the desk as she walked into the office. 'I've just had some news,' she told him. 'Someone's interested in the house.'

'Will they make an offer?' He dropped his pen on the desk and sat back, his dark eyes seeking hers.

'Yes, it's possible. They want to turn Tilly House into a health spa.'

Since his return last night they had barely spoken. She'd told him that Jon had left, but his comments had been brief and he hadn't breathed a word about Venetia.

'A health spa?' His forehead pleated as he looked up at her.

'With lots of renovations,' she added with a short laugh. 'You can imagine it, can't you?'

'Yes,' he answered her darkly. 'I can.'

'I suppose it's all for the best,' she said brightly. 'And, anyway, I'd like to exchange contracts before I leave.'

He raised an eyebrow. 'And when—exactly—will that be?'

'My flight's scheduled for the second week in September.'

'A month and a bit,' he calculated, and she watched the little muscles work in his jaw. His eyes darkened and he cleared his throat. 'That doesn't leave much time.'

'No, but enough to close the surgery and have everyone transferred to Greg—just until you're open next door.'

He nodded again. 'If all goes well—December.'

'Christmas,' she murmured, and swallowed.

His eyes twisted briefly with hers and she felt her heart leap. If only they could stop this ridiculous charade. Even if he talked about Venetia, even if he told her that he was going to marry the wretched girl, it would put an end to the misery of not knowing.

What had she done so wrong that he couldn't be honest with her? Then she realised she was looking at the top of his head as he bent to concentrate on whatever it was that needed his attention so urgently. And she dragged herself off before she made a complete fool of herself—again.

Abbie ploughed through a surprisingly busy month of surgeries. The world and his wife attended—all wishing her well and sorry that she was going. The consensus of opinion on the polyclinic was favourable. She knew she would have no worries about her patients being looked after, though she did have reservations about the house. Not that she was going to refuse the offer the health spa clients had made. She'd accepted and tried to come to terms with the fact that things had to change.

Even Tilly House.

Despite the busy surgeries, her mind kept tagging onto her missed period. If she missed the next one towards the end of August, she would make a test. What would she do if she was pregnant? The thought of an abortion made her heave. Yet she was going back to the States to continue her career. Telling Cas was out of the question. Their 'mistake' hadn't been referred to again. They were polite, but distant. It was a kind of truce and she kept to it. What else could she do?

Towards the end of August, Susan Dunning came to see Abbie. She had met Ralf and was eager to tell Abbie her news.

'We're taking things slowly,' she admitted, 'but we want our relationship to work for Joanne's sake. I've been given a place in September—one of those little terraced houses in Tilly. It would be lovely if we could move in as a family.'

Abbie felt Susan had a decent chance of happiness and since Josie was to be discharged, the Dunnings would have their lives back again. Reggie Donaldson had conquered his panic attacks and had had a successful laryngoscopy. The results had been cleared by the hospital and he called in to let Abbie know. 'Not that I'll be doing this yoga lark for much longer,' he told her when out of earshot of his wife. 'I don't mind a bit of deep breathing, but I draw the line at tying myself in knots. I'll leave that to the missus.'

Even Howard sent them a card from Disneyland. He sounded fit and well and the only goodbyes left to say were to Eve and Charlie.

'I'll phone you,' Charlie said on her last day. 'I'm not very good at writing.' She hugged Cas and gave Abbie a little brooch. 'Just to remember me by,' she sniffed.

And when Abbie visited Eve after Charlie had gone back to London, Eve, with the wisdom of her years, guessed the truth, which Abbie's pregnancy test had only just confirmed.

'Are you certain you're making the right decision?' Eve asked as they sat in the garden. 'For you—and the baby?'

Abbie stared at Eve. 'How do you know about the baby?'

Eve patted her hand. 'Intuition, my dear—and a little logic. Last time we spoke you were deeply unhappy, despite your brave words. And knowing you as I do, I guessed the problem was complicated. And I was right, wasn't I?'

Abbie nodded. 'Yes, I've already taken a test. I'm pregnant.'

Eve leaned forward and squeezed her hand. 'Abbie, dear, don't do anything you'll regret. Talk to Caspar—tell him what's happened.'

Abbie shook her head stubbornly. 'Oh, no doubt he would do the right thing—for the baby's sake. But he's already admitted our relationship is a mistake. I don't want to make another one, Eve. Pity would be cold comfort.'

It had been a sad and poignant little conversation. Their parting was painful, though Abbie promised to write. When Abbie arrived home, a large haulage van had arrived and the men were waiting to take the last of the furniture into storage.

The house looked desolate. The marks on the walls and the bare boards recorded the passage of years, the events of her childhood now chronicled by shadows. Abbie felt like a traitor, as if she were leaving a sinking ship.

It was all she could do to continue with the surgeries, and when at last September arrived, she gave them up altogether.

'Would you mind doing the last week or two?' she asked Cas.

'No,' he told her. 'But is there a reason?'

'I have things to do,' she lied. 'Loose ends to tie up.'

'If that's what you want.' He shrugged and said no more and they returned to the polite truce that had been forged between them.

She was beginning to feel sick in the mornings, a niggle of nausea that cramped her stomach and made her retch. She knew she was pale and did her best to hide it, but there was no way she could eat breakfast.

Three days before she was due to leave she gave Cas the keys of her father's car. 'It's the only thing left,' she told him. 'I should have sold it, but there hasn't really been time.'

'What do you want me to do with it?' he asked her.

'Find it a home,' she suggested. 'Or, I suppose, scrap it.'

'A pity.' He frowned. 'Your father loved that car.'

Which was why she hadn't been able to sell it, of course. But she didn't answer and they stood for a moment in silence in the front garden as the first gentle breeze of autumn swirled the dead leaves at their feet. The workmen next door had made a bonfire and the smell drifted over the hedge. It was a gorgeous September day and Abbie looked up into Cas's face.

He was staring at her and she wondered how she was going to get through the weekend. Her stomach tilted, and she swallowed and hoped she didn't look as fragile as she felt. She smiled brightly and glanced over the hedge.

'Do you want to show me around—one last time?'

He looked surprised but he smiled and they walked together down the drive and into the lane. Little flashes of the past few months came into her mind, and as they entered the new building her heart gave a little start. It was beautiful, spacious and elegant. The long low roof was in keeping with the discreet and modern style, and she saw at once that the ugly duckling had become a swan.

'I'll show you the rooms if you like,' he told her, and helped her navigate her way through and pushed doors ajar for her to see in. They walked the passages of the ground floor and then up the stairs to the first, and from a window she saw Tilly House. He stood behind her and they gazed across. The late summer sun sparkled on her bedroom window.

A lump formed in her throat and she turned away quickly. When Cas asked her if she'd like to cross to the extension but said that it wasn't quite finished, she shook her head.

'Perhaps another day,' she said, and he nodded.

But she knew there wouldn't be another day. This, for her, was the end. Tomorrow she would leave, two days ahead of time, so avoiding the last and most difficult goodbye.

CHAPTER FOURTEEN

THE two nights Abbie spent in the hotel left her feeling low, but it was better than having to say goodbye to Cas—and wait all weekend to say it.

Instead, she'd written him a letter, brief and to the point. She needed to do some shopping in London, she'd said, and had decided to leave earlier than planned. She had thanked him and said she would write…

But they both knew she wouldn't. There was nothing left in Tilly for her. The house would soon be gone, the last roots of her life in England.

And Cas? Somehow she'd survive. She was going to have this baby and try to pick up the pieces of her life in LA. She would cope for the baby's sake. And they would live without him.

The airport lounge was thronged as Abbie tried to keep down the cup of tea that she'd sipped an hour ago. It was swirling perilously near to her throat and she didn't know if she was going to make it to the gate.

Suddenly everyone was moving and she was on her feet and trying to make her way towards the queue. Her head was spinning. She tried to focus. A merry-go-round was playing and she was on it, her heart leaping and perspiration beading her forehead.

She was leaving England. There was no turning back now. A few more steps and she would be through Customs and on the plane, her life in England over.

'Are you all right?' a voice said beside her. A man with a raincoat over his arm was staring at her pale, drawn face, concern in his eyes.

'Yes.' She nodded. 'I'm OK, thanks.'

'I'm the same every time.' He smiled. 'Nerves always get the better of me.'

She nodded and tried to return his smile, but the top of her head seemed to be revolving. His face was a muzzy grey, but she saw him turn and walk on. Then her stomach did a full loop the loop and there was blackness as her legs gave way and she crumpled to the floor.

'Abbie?' The voice floated around her, soothed against her cheek and rippled like silk over her skin. 'Abbie, darling…'

If this was a dream, she found herself thinking, she wanted it to go on. The voice was Cas's and he was so close she could feel him. Feel his breath and smell his smell. And if she reached out, she would touch his skin…just like the dream she'd had before.

'Abbie…?' he said again.

Her eyelids flickered and she lifted them slowly. She was certain she would see the man with the mac. Instead, she saw a pair of deep brown eyes which might be mistaken for black if you didn't know the owner very well. And you hadn't looked into them as deeply as she had. Her fingers reached up for the soft, dark hair that touched his collar, and it was there. As real, as thick and beautiful as it was in reality.

'Where am I?' she faltered, and tried to sit up.

'Darling, it's all right. We're in one of the rest rooms at the airport.'

'Cas? You're here—really here?'

'By the skin of my teeth.' He held a glass of water to her lips. 'Drink this. Slowly.' She sipped and lay back, movement exhausting her. He put the glass down and touched the edge of her lips tenderly with his finger. 'What am I going to do with you?' he sighed, and bent forward, lowering his head until his mouth touched hers and trapped her lips. 'Unfortunately, my options are limited,' he murmured. 'At least whilst you're in this state.'

'Did I faint?'

'You fainted—fortunately. Otherwise you'd be on that plane by now. You and our baby. Winging your way above the clouds and out of my reach.'

Abbie's lids flew open. 'Cas—you *know*?'

He nodded, his dark eyes flaying her. 'Thanks to some revealing evidence I found in your bedroom. All those books and magazines that clearly showed your interest in, or should I say *obsession* with, pregnancy?' His eyes were soft and despairing. 'Oh, Abbie, I'm right, aren't I? I'm going to be a father? Please, don't disappoint me!'

She nodded wordlessly and he pulled her against him, the sigh that was trapped deep in his chest only escaping as he let it out slowly, holding onto his control.

'I...I couldn't tell you...' she fumbled. 'I just couldn't.'

'But why, my darling, why?'

'I wanted to, but...well, I thought you might stay with me for the baby's sake, not because... because...'

He held her away slowly, his face tight with emotion. 'Abbie, what was going on in that stubborn little mind of yours? I love you, don't you know that by now? I love you.'

'Oh, Cas, do you—really?'

'Why do you think I drove up here like a maniac to find you? Thank God I knew the time of your flight, but even so it was a damn close thing. How could you leave me, Abbie?'

Her eyes filled with tears. 'You said…you said what happened between us was a mistake—'

'I was angry,' he growled, cutting her short as he trapped a stray lock of hair and wound it behind her ear. 'And jealous of Jon Kirk.'

'That's ridiculous,' she croaked. 'Jon is just a friend.'

'The man is crazy about you.'

She reached out to touch his cheek and smiled softly. 'Jon might have made it sound like a grand romance. But it isn't—wasn't—and never has been.'

'He was convincing,' Cas told her soberly, 'when he phoned that morning. We'd slept the whole night in each other's arms. Then those things he said…about missing you, wanting to take you back to the US…they simply shattered me.'

'Oh, Cas…I'm sorry. I should have made it clear he meant nothing to me, but you kept talking about Venetia. I was so jealous.'

'Jealous of *Venetia*?' He laughed softly, crooking an eyebrow. 'Well, you had no need to be.'

'She's very lovely, Cas.'

He rolled his eyes. 'Not quite the word I'd use. Persistent perhaps, or irritating or even a wretched nuisance.'

'But she said—'

'I met Venetia,' Cas interrupted her firmly, 'a few years ago when I unwisely made up a four-some as a favour to a friend. It was, of course, a disaster. I should never have been persuaded into it. I had nothing in common with her—or her with me. However, the more I tried to avoid her, the more she kept appearing. Even in Tilly where, as you know, she wreaked havoc. And thanks to you and your suggestion that I should take her out...it nearly happened all over again...' He left his sentence unfinished as Abbie began to laugh.

'Oh, Cas, I'm sorry.'

He grinned. 'So you should be. I wasn't think-ing rationally. I couldn't defend myself.' He bent and covered her lips with soft, butterfly kisses. 'I'd just fallen in love.'

'But I didn't know that,' she reminded him, grateful he couldn't witness her blush. 'I thought you were going to stay with Venetia in London...and...' She looked under her lashes. 'I did see you put a gorgeous bouquet of roses into the back of the car.'

'Did you now?' He smiled ruefully. 'Well, I came to London to see the architect, to finalise the changes on the clinic. Not to see Venetia. And the roses—they were for you, but you made me take Venetia out and by the time I got back they had wilted away.'

Abbie flung her arms around him. 'Oh, Cas. I've been so stupid.'

He cradled her against him. 'Abbie, don't ever leave me again.'

She stared into his eyes. Gorgeous, sexy brown eyes that had her swallowing hard. 'Cas, do you really want this baby?'

'More than anything else in the world,' he told her, his voice roughened with emotion. 'I want us to be a family. To live and work together, through good times and bad. I've always wanted it, Abbie. From the first moment I saw you.' He placed his hand on her stomach and curved his fingers. 'This is going to be the most loved child in all the world. And we're going to live in the most beautiful place in all the world. Tilly House.'

Abbie's green eyes widened. 'But Tilly House has been sold, Cas.'

'No, it hasn't.' He smiled deviously. 'Not now they've discovered the untenable subsidence and massive dry rot.'

'But there isn't any!' she exclaimed.

'Oh, yes, there is. If you look in the right places.'

She gave a gurgle of joy and then he was kissing her and tangling his hands in her hair, and as she closed her eyes and lay back, all she could think was, *Please, don't let anyone come in.*

Not yet…

MEDICAL ROMANCE™

Large Print

Titles for the next six months…

January

EMERGENCY GROOM	Josie Metcalfe
HIS BROTHER'S SON	Jennifer Taylor
THE DOCTOR'S MISTRESS	Lilian Darcy
DR PRESTON'S DAUGHTER	Laura MacDonald

February

ACCIDENTAL SEDUCTION	Caroline Anderson
THE SPANISH DOCTOR	Margaret Barker
THE ER AFFAIR	Leah Martyn
EMERGENCY: DOCTOR IN NEED	Lucy Clark

March

A DOCTOR'S HONOUR	Jessica Matthews
A FAMILY OF THEIR OWN	Jennifer Taylor
PARAMEDIC PARTNERS	Abigail Gordon
A DOCTOR'S COURAGE	Gill Sanderson

MILLS & BOON®

1202 LP 2P P1 Medical

MEDICAL ROMANCE™

Large Print

April

MORE THAN CARING — Josie Metcalfe
HER UNEXPECTED FAMILY — Gill Sanderson
THE VISITING SURGEON — Lucy Clark
THE DOCTOR'S RUNAWAY BRIDE — Sarah Morgan

May

CHRISTMAS KNIGHT — Meredith Webber
A MOTHER FOR HIS CHILD — Lilian Darcy
THE IRRESISTIBLE DOCTOR — Carol Wood
POLICE DOCTOR — Laura MacDonald

June

ASSIGNMENT: SINGLE FATHER — Caroline Anderson
MORE THAN A GIFT — Josie Metcalfe
DR BLAKE'S ANGEL — Marion Lennox
HOME BY CHRISTMAS — Jennifer Taylor

MILLS & BOON®

1202 LP 2P P2 Medica